A SUMMER IN A CAÑON

A CALIFORNIA STORY

BY

KATE DOUGLAS WIGGIN

AUTHOR OF "THE BIRDS' CHRISTMAS CAROL," "THE STORY OF PATSY," ETC.

BOSTON AND NEW YORK
HOUGHTON, MIFFLIN AND COMPANY
The Riverside Press, Cambridge
1898

The Riverside Press, Cambridge, Mass., U. S. A.
Electrotyped and Printed by H. O. Houghton & Co.

CONTENTS.

CHAPTER IX.

CHAPTER X.

CHAPTER XI.

SCENE: *A Camping Ground in the Cañon Las Flores.*

PEOPLE IN THE TENTS.

DR. PAUL WINSHIP	*Mine Host.*
MRS. TRUTH WINSHIP	*The Guardian Angel.*
DICKY WINSHIP	*A Small Scamp of Six Years.*
BELL WINSHIP	*The Camp Poetess.*
POLLY OLIVER	*A Sweet but Saucy Lass.*
MARGERY NOBLE	*A Nut-Brown Mayde.*
PHILIP NOBLE	*The Useful Member.*
GEOFFREY STRONG	*A Harvard Boy.*
JACK HOWARD	*Prince of Mischief*
HOP YET	*A Heathen Chinee.*
PANCHO GUTIERREZ	*A Mexican man-of-all-work.*

CHAPTER I.

PREPARATION AND DEPARTURE.

"One to make ready, and two to prepare."

IT was nine o'clock one sunny California morning, and Geoffrey Strong stood under the live-oak trees in Las Flores Cañon, with a pot of black paint in one hand and a huge brush in the other. He could have handled these implements to better purpose and with better grace had not his arms been firmly held by three laughing girls, who pulled not wisely, but too well. He was further incommoded by the presence of a small urchin who lay on the

dusty ground beneath his feet, fastening an
upward clutch on the legs of his trousers.

There were three large canvas tents directly
in front of them, yet no one of these seemed
to be the object of dissension, but rather a redwood board, some three feet in length, which
was nailed on a tree near by.

"Camp Frolic! Please let us name it Camp
Frolic!" cried Bell Winship, with a persuasive
twitch of her cousin's sleeve.

"No, no; not Camp Frolic," pleaded Polly
Oliver. "Pray, pray let us have Camp Ha-Ha;
my heart is set upon it."

"As you are Strong, be merciful," quoted
Margery Noble, coaxingly; "take my advice
and call it Harmony Camp."

At this juncture, a lovely woman, whose
sweet face and smile made you love her at
once, came up the hill from the brookside.
"What, what! still quarreling, children?"
she asked, laughingly. "Let me be peacemaker.
I've just asked the Doctor for a name, and he
suggests Camp Chaparral. What do you say?"

Bell released one coat-tail. "That isn't
wholly bad," she said, critically, while the
other girls clapped their hands with approval;
for anything that aunt Truth suggested was
sure to be quite right.

"Wait a minute, good people," cried Jack Howard, flinging his fishing tackle under a tree and sauntering toward the scene of action. "Suppose we have a referee, a wise and noble judge. Call Hop Yet, and let him decide this all-important subject."

His name being sung and shouted in various keys by the assembled company, Hop Yet appeared at the door of the brush kitchen, a broad grin on his countenance, a plucked fowl in his hand.

Geoffrey took the floor. "Now, Hop Yet, you know I got name, you got name, everybody got name. We want name this camp: you sabe? Miss Bell, she say Camp Frolic. Frolic all same heap good time" (here he executed a sort of war-dance which was intended to express wild joy). "Miss Pauline, she say Camp Ha-Ha, big laugh: sabe? Ha! ha! ha! ha! ha! ha!" (chorus joined in by all to fully illustrate the subject). "Miss Madge, she say Camp Harmony. Harmony all same heap quiet time, plenty eat, plenty drink, plenty sleep, no fight, no too muchee talk. Mrs. Winship, she say Camp Chaparral: you sabe? Chaparral, Hop Yet. Now what you say?"

Hop Yet seemed to regard the question with mingled embarrassment and amusement, but

being a sharp and talkative Chinaman gave
his answer promptly : " Me say Camp Chap-lal
heap good name; plenty chap-lal all lound; me
hang um dish-cloth, tow'l, little boy's stockin',
on chap-lal; all same clo'se-line velly good.
Miss Bell she flolic, Miss Polly she ha! ha!
allee same Camp Chap-lal."

And so Camp Chaparral it was; the redwood
board flaunted the assertion before the eyes of
the public (which was a rather limited one, to
be sure) in less than half an hour, and the
artist, after painting the words in rustic letters
a foot long, cut branches of the stiff, ungracious bushes and nailed them to the tree in
confirmation and illustration of the fact. He
then carefully deposited the paint-pot in a
secret place, where it might be out of sight
and touch of a certain searching eye and mischievous hand well known and feared of him;
but before the setting sun had dropped below
the line of purple mountain tops, a small boy,
who will be known in these annals as Dicky
Winship, might have been seen sitting on the
empty paint-pot, while from a dingy pool upon
the ground he was attempting to paint a copy
of the aforesaid inscription upon the side of a
too patient goat, who saw no harm in the operation. He was alone and very, very happy.

And now I must tell you the way in which all this began. You may not realize it, dear young folks, but this method of telling a story is very much the fashion with grown-up people, and of course I am not to blame, since I did n't begin it.

The plan is this: You must first write a chapter showing all your people, men, women, children, dogs, and cats, in a certain place, doing certain things. Then you must go back a year or two and explain how they all happen to be there. Perhaps you may have to drag your readers twenty-five years into the regions of the past, and show them the first tooth of your oldest character; but that does n't matter a bit, — the further the better. Then, when everybody has forgotten what came to pass in the first chapter, you are ready to take it up again, as if there had never been any parenthesis. However, I shall not introduce you to the cradles, cribs, or trundle-beds of my merry young campers, but merely ask you to retrace your steps one week, and look upon them in their homes.

On one of the pleasantest streets of a certain little California town stood, and still stands for aught I know, a pretty brown cottage, with its verandas covered with passion-

vine and a brilliant rose-garden in front. It
is picturesque enough to attract the attention
of any passer-by, and if you had chosen to
peep through the crevices in the thick vines
and look in at the open window, you might
have thought it lovelier within than without.

It was a bright day, and the gracious June
sunshine flooded the room with yellow light.
Three young girls, perhaps fourteen or fifteen
years old, were seated in different parts of the
large room, plying industrious crochet needles
and tatting shuttles. Three pairs of bright
eyes were dancing with fun and gladness; and
another pair, the softest and clearest of all,
looked out from a broad white bed in the corner, — tired eyes, and oh, so patient, for the
health-giving breezes wafted in from the blue
ocean and carried over mountain tops and vine-
covered slopes had so far failed to bring back
Elsie Howard's strength and vigor.

The graceful, brown-haired girl, with the
bright, laughter-loving face, was Bell Winship.
She of the dancing blue eyes, pink cheeks, and
reckless little sun-bonnet was Pauline, otherwise
Polly Oliver. Did you ever know a Polly
without some one of these things? Well,
my Polly had them all, and, besides, a saucy
freckled nose, a crown of fluffy, reddish-yellow

hair, and a shower of coaxing little pitfalls called dimples round her pretty mouth. She made you think of a sunbeam, a morning song-bird, a dancing butterfly, or an impetuous little crocus just out after the first spring shower. Dislike her? You could n't. Approve of her? You would n't always. Love her? Of course; you could n't help yourself, — I defy you.

To be sure, if you prefer a quiet life, and do not want to be led into exploits of all kinds, invariably beginning with risk, attended with danger, and culminating in despair, you had better not engage in an intimate friendship with Miss Pauline Oliver, but fix your affections on the quiet, thoughtful, but not less lovable girl who sits by the bedside stroking Elsie Howard's thin white hand. Nevertheless, I am obliged to state that Margery Noble herself, earnest, demure, and given to reflection, was Polly's willing slave and victim. However, I 've forgotten to tell you that Polly was as open and frank as the daylight, at once torrid and con-stant in her affections, brave, self-forgetting as well as self-willed; and that though she did have a tongue just the least bit saucy, she used it valiantly in the defense of others. "She 'll come out all right," said a dear old-fashioned grandfather of hers whom she had left way back in a Vermont farmhouse. "She's got to be purged o' considerable dross, but she'll come out pure gold, I tell you."

Pretty, wise, tender Margery Noble, with her sleek brown braids, her innocent, questioning eyes, her soft voice, willing hands, and shy, quiet manners! "She will either end as the matron of an orphan asylum or as head nurse in a hospital." So Bell Winship often used to say; but then she was chiefly celebrated for talking nonsense, and nobody ever paid much attention to her. But if you should crave a breath of fresh air, or want to believe that the spring has come, just call Bell Winship in, as she walks with her breezy step down the street. Her very hair seems instinct with life, with its flying tendrils of bronze brightness and the riotous little curls on her brow and temples. Then, too, she has a particularly jaunty way of putting on her jacket, or wearing a flower or a ribbon; and as for her ringing peal of laughter, it is like a chime of silver bells.

Elsie Howard, the invalid friend of the girls, was as dear to them as they were to each other. She kept the secrets of the "firm;" mourned over their griefs and smiled over their joys; was proud of their talents and tenderly blind to their faults. The little wicker rocking-chair

by the bedside was often made a sort of con-
fessional, at which she presided, the tenderest
and most sympathetic little priestess in the universe ; and every afternoon the piazza, with its
lattice of green vines, served as a mimic throne-
room, where she was wont to hold high court,
surrounded by her devoted subjects. Here
Geoffrey Strong used often to read to the assembled company " David Copperfield," " Alice
in Wonderland," or snatches from the maga-
zines, while Jack Howard lazily stretched himself under the orange-trees and braided lariats,
a favorite occupation with California boys.
About four o'clock Philip Noble would ride
up from his father's fruit ranch, some three
miles out on the San Marcos road, and, hitching his little sorrel mare Chispa at the gate,
stay an hour before going to the post-office.

This particular afternoon, however, was not
one of Elsie's bright ones, and there was no
sign of court or invalid queen on the piazza.
The voices of the girls floated out from Elsie's
bedroom, while the boys, too, seemed to be
somewhere in the vicinity, for there was a constant stirring about as of lively preparation,
together with noise of hammering and sawing.

" If you were only going, Elsie, our cup of
happiness would be full," sighed Bell.

"Not only would it be full, Bell, but it would be running over, and we should positively stand in the slop," said Polly. "No, you need n't frown at me, miss; that expression is borrowed from no less a person than Sydney Smith."

"Don't think any more about me," smiled Elsie. "Perhaps I can come down in the course of the summer. I know it will be the happiest time in the world, but I don't envy you a bit; in fact, I 'm very glad you 're going, because you 'll have such a lovely budget of adventures to tell me when you come back."

"When we come back, indeed!" exclaimed Bell. "Why, we shall write long round-robin letters every few days, and send them by the team. Papa says Pancho will have to go over to the stage station at least once a week for letters and any provisions we may need."

"Oh, won't that be delightful, — almost as good as being there myself! And, Margery dear, you must make them tell me every least little thing that happens. You know they are such fly-aways that they 'll only write me when they learn to swim, or shoot a wildcat, or get lost in the woods. I want to know all the stupid bits : what you have for dinner, how and where you sleep, how your camp looks, what you do from morning till night, and how Dicky behaves."

"I can tell you that beforehand," said Bell, dolefully. "Jack will shoot him by mistake on Thursday; he will be kicked by the horses Friday, and bitten by tarantulas and rattlesnakes Saturday; he will eat poison oak on Sunday, get lost in the cañon Monday, be eaten by a bear Tuesday, and drowned in the pool Wednesday. These incidents will complete his first week; and if they produce no effect on his naturally strong constitution, he will treat us to another week, containing just as many mishaps, but no duplicates."

By the time this dismal prophecy was ended the other girls were in a breathless fit of laughter, though all acknowledged it was likely to be fulfilled.

"I went over the camping-ground last summer," said Margery. "You know it is quite near papa's sheep ranch, and it is certainly the most beautiful place in California. The tents will be pitched at the mouth of the cañon, where there is a view of the ocean, and just at the back will be a lovely grove of wild oaks and sycamore-trees."

"Oh, won't it be delicious!" sighed Elsie. "I feel as if I could sniff the air this minute. But there! I won't pretend that I'm dying for fresh air, with the breath of the sea coming in

at my south window, and a whiff of jasmine
and honeysuckle from the piazza. That would
be nonsense. Are your trunks packed?"

"Trunks!" exclaimed Polly. "Would you
believe it, our clothes are packed in gunny-
sacks! We start in our camping-dresses, with
ulsters for the steamer and dusters for the long
drive. Then we each have — let me see what
we have: a short, tough riding-skirt with a
jersey, a bathing-dress, and some gingham
morning-gowns to wear about the camp at
breakfast time."

"And flannel gowns for the night, and two
pairs of boots, and a riding-cap and one hat
apiece," added Margery.

"But oh, Elsie, my dear, you should see
Dicky in his camping-suits," laughed Bell.
"They are a triumph of invention on mamma's
part. Just imagine! one is of some enameled
cloth that was left over from the new carriage
cushions; it is very shiny and elegant; and the
other, truly, is of soft tanned leather, and just
as pretty as it can be. Then he has hob-nailed,
copper-toed boots, and a hat that ties under his
chin. Poor little man, he has lost his curls,
too, and looks rather like a convict."

Mrs. Howard came in the door while Bell
was speaking, and laughed heartily at the

description of Dicky's curious outfit. "What time do you start?" she asked, as she laid a bunch of mignonette on Elsie's table.

"At eleven to-morrow morning," Bell answered. "Everything is packed. We are to start in the steamer, and when we come to our old landing, about forty miles down the coast, we are to get off and take a three-seated thorough-brace wagon, and drive over to Las Flores Cañon. Pancho has hired a funny little pack mule; he says we shall need one in going up the mountain, and that the boys can take him when they go out shooting, — to carry the deer home, you know."

"If I can bring Elsie down, as I hope, we must come by land," said Mrs. Howard. "I thought we could take two days for the journey, sleeping at the Burtons' ranch on the way. The doctor says that if she can get strength enough to bear the ride, the open-air life will do her good, even if she does nothing but lie in the hammock."

"And be waited upon by six willing slaves," added Polly.

"And be fed on canned corned beef and tomato stew," laughed Bell.

"Not a bit of it," said Margery. "Hop Yet is a splendid cook, if he has anything to cook,

and we 'll feed her on broiled tidbits of baby
venison, goat's milk, wild bees' honey, and cunning little mourning doves, roasted on a spit."

"Good gracious," cried Bell, "what angels'
food! only I would as soon devour a pet canary
as a mourning dove. But to think that I 've
been trying to diet for a week in order to get
intimate with suffering and privation! Polly
came to stay with me one night, and we slept
on the floor, with only a blanket under us, and
no pillow; it was perfectly horrid. Polly
dreamed that her grandfather ate up her grand-
mother, and I that Dicky stabbed the Jersey
calf with a pickle-fork."

"Horrors!" ejaculated Margery; "that 's a
pleasant prospect for your future bedfellows.
I hope the gophers won't make you nervous,
gnawing and scratching in the straw; I got
used to them last summer. But we really
must go, darling," and she stooped to kiss Elsie
good-by.

"Well, I suppose you ought," she answered.
"But remember you are to start from this gate;
aunt Truth has promised me the fun of seeing
you out of sight."

The girls went out at a side door, and joined
the boys, who were busily at work cleaning
their guns on the broad western porch.

"How are you coming on?" questioned Polly.

"Oh, finely," answered Jack, who always constituted himself chief spokesman, unless driven from the rostrum by some one possessed of a nimbler tongue. "I only hope your feminine togs are in half as good order."

"We take no baggage to speak of," said Bell, loftily. "Papa has cut us down to the very last notch, and says the law allows very few pounds on this trip."

"The less the better," quoth Geoff cheerily; "then you'll have to polish up your mental jewels."

"Which you consider imitation, I suppose," sniffed Polly.

"Perish the thought!" cried Jack. "But, speaking of mental jewels, you should see the arrangements Geoff has made for polishing his. He has actually stuck in six large volumes, any one of which would be a remedy for sleeplessness. What are you going to study, Miss Pol-y-on-o-mous Oliver?"

"Now, Jack, let us decide at once whether you intend to be respectful or not. I don't propose to expose myself to your nonsense for two months unless you make me good promises."

"Why, that wasn't disrespectful. It is my

newest word, and it simply means having many titles. I'm sure you have more than most people."

"Very well, then! I'll overlook the irreverence this time, and announce that I shall not take anything whatever to read, but simply reflect upon what I know already."

"That may last for the first week," said Bell, slyly, "but what will you do afterward?"

"I'll reflect upon what you don't know," retorted Polly. "That will easily occupy me two months."

Fortunately, at the very moment this stinging remark was made, Phil Noble dashed up to the front gate, flung his bridle over the hitching-post, and lifted his hat from a very warm brow.

"Hail, chief of the commissary department!" cried Geoffrey, with mock salute. "Have you dispatched the team?"

"Yes; everything is all right," said Phil, breathlessly, delivering himself of his information in spasmodic bursts of words. "Such a lot of work it was! here's the list. Pancho will dump them on the ground and let us settle them when we get there. Such a load! You should have seen it! Hardly room for him to sit up in front with the Chinaman. Just hear this," and he drew a large document from what Polly called " a back-stairs pocket." "Forty cans corned beef, four guns, three Dutch cheeses, pickles, fishing tackle, flour, bacon, three bushels onions, crate of dishes, Jack's banjo, potatoes, ' Short History of the English People,' cooking utensils, three hair pillows, box of ginger-snaps, four hammocks, coffee, cartridges, sugar, ' Macaulay's Essays,' Pond's extract, sixteen hams, Bell's guitar, pop-corn, molasses, salt, St. Jacob's oil, ' Conquest of Mexico,' sack of almonds, flea powder, and smoked herring. Whew! I packed them all myself."

" In precisely that order ? " questioned Polly.

" In precisely that order, Miss Oliver," returned Phil, urbanely. " Any one who feels that said packing might be improved upon has only to mount the fleet Arabian yonder " (the animal alluded to seized this moment to stand on three legs, hang his head, and look dejected), " and, giving him the rein, speed o'er the trackless plain which leads to San Miguel, o'ertake the team, and re-pack the contents according to her own satisfaction."

" No butter, nor eggs, nor fresh vegetables ? " asked Margery. " We shall starve ! "

" Not at all," quoth Jack. " Polly will grace-

fully dispose a horse-blanket about her shoulders, to shield her from the chill dews of the
early morn, mount the pack mule exactly at
cock-crow every day, and ride to a neighboring
ranch where there are tons of the aforesaid
articles awaiting our consumption."

"Can you see me doing it, girls? Does it
seem entirely natural?" asked Polly, with great
gravity.

"Now hear my report as chairman of the committee of arrangements," said Geoffrey Strong,
seating himself with dignity on a barrel of
nails. "The tents, ropes, tool-boxes, bed-sacks,
blankets, furniture, etc., all went down on
Monday's steamer, and I have a telegram from
Larry's Landing saying that they arrived in
good order, and that a Mexican gentleman who
owns a mammoth wood-cart will take them up
to-morrow when we go ourselves. The procession will move at one P. M., wind and weather
permitting, in the following order : —

"1. Chief Noble on his gallant broncho.

"2. Commander Strong on his ditto, ditto.

"3. Main conveyance or triumphal chariot,
driven by Aid-de-Camp John Howard, and car-
rying Dr. and Mrs. Winship, our most worship-
ful and benignant host and hostess; Master
Dick Winship, the heir apparent; three other

young persons not worth mentioning; and four cans of best leaf lard, which I omitted to put with the other provisions.

" 4. Wood-cart containing baggage, driven by Señor Don Manuel Felipe Hilario Noriega from Dead Wood Gulch.

" 5. One small tan terrier."

" Oh, Geoff, Geoff, pray do stop! it's too much ! " cried the girls in a fit of laughter.

" Hurrah ! " shouted Jack, tossing his hat into a tall eucalyptus-tree in his excitement. " Tent life forever ! "

" Good-by, ye pomps and vanities ! " chanted Bell, kissing her hand in imaginary farewell. " Verily the noisy city shall know us no more, for we depart for the green forests."

" And the city will not be as noisy *when* you depart," murmured Jack, with an impudence that luckily passed unnoticed.

" If Elsie could only come too ! " sighed Polly.

Wednesday morning dawned as bright and beautiful as all mornings are wont to dawn in Southern California. A light mist hung over the old adobe mission church, through which, with its snow-white towers and cold, clear-cut lines, it rose like a frozen fairy castle. Bell

opened her sleepy eyes with the very earliest
birds, and running to the little oval window,
framed with white-rose vines, looked out at
the new day just creeping up into the world.

"O dear and beautiful home of mine, how
charming, how charming you are! I wonder
if you are not really Paradise!" she said,
dreamily; and the marvel is that the rising sun
did not stop a moment in sheer surprise at the
sight of this radiant morning vision; for the
oval window opening to the east was a pretty
frame, with its outline marked by the dewy rose-
vine covered with hundreds of pure, half-opened
buds and swaying tendrils, and she stood there
in it, a fair image of the morning in her innocent white gown. Her luminous eyes still
mirrored the shadowy visions of dreamland,
mingled with dancing lights of hope and joyful
anticipation; while on her fresh cheeks, which
had not yet lost the roundness of childhood,
there glowed, as in the eastern skies, the faint
pink blush of the morning.

The town is yet asleep, and in truth it is
never apt to be fairly wide awake. The air is
soft and balmy; the lovely Pacific, a quivering,
sparkling sheet of blue and gray and green
flecked with white foam, stretches far out
until it is lost in the rosy sky; and the moun-

tains, all purple and pink and faint crimson and gray, stand like sentinels along the shore. The scent of the roses, violets, and mignonette mingled with the cloying fragrance of the datura is heavy in the still air. The bending, willowy pepper-trees show myriad bunches of yellow blossoms, crimson seed-berries, and fresh green leaves, whose surface, not rain-washed for months, is as full of color as ever. The palm-trees rise without a branch, tall, slender, and graceful, from the warmly generous earth, and spread at last, as if tired of their straightness, into beautiful crowns of fans, which sway toward each other with every breath of air. Innumerable butterflies and humming-birds, in the hot, dazzling sunshine of noonday, will be hovering over the beds of sweet purple heliotrope and finding their way into the hearts of the passion-flowers, but as yet not the faintest whir of wings can be heard. Looking eastward or westward, you see either brown foot-hills, or, a little later on, emerald slopes whose vines hang heavy with the half-ripened grapes.

And hark! A silvery note strikes on the dewy stillness. It is the mission bell, ringing for morning mass; and if you look yonder, you may see the Franciscan friars going to prayers, with their loose gray gowns, their girdle of

rope, their sandaled feet, and their jingling
rosaries ; and perhaps a Spanish señorita, with
her trailing dress, and black shawl loosely
thrown over her head, from out the folds of
which her two dark eyes burn like gleaming
fires.   A solitary Mexican gallops by, with
gayly decorated saddle and heavily laden sad-
dle-bags hanging from it ; perhaps he is taking
home provisions to his wife and dark-eyed
babies who live up in a little dimple of the
mountain side, almost hidden from sight by the
olive-trees.   And then a patient, hardy little
mustang lopes along the street, bearing on his
back three laughing boys, one behind the other,
on a morning ride into town from the *mesa*.

The mist has floated away from the old mission now, the sun has climbed a little higher,
and Bell has come away from the window in a
gentle mood.

"Oh, Polly, I don't see how anybody can be
wicked in such a beautiful, beautiful world."

"Humph !" said Polly, dipping her curly
head deep into the water-bowl, and coming up
looking like a little drowned kitten.   "When
you want to be hateful, you don't stop to think
whether you're looking at a cactus or a rose-
bush, do you ? "

"Very true," sighed Bell, quite silenced by

this practical illustration. " Now I 'll try the effect of the landscape on my temper by dressing Dicky, while he dances about the room and plays with his tan terrier."

But it happened that Dicky was on his very best behavior, and stood as still as a sign-post while being dressed. It is true he ate a couple of matches and tumbled down-stairs twice before breakfast, so that after that hurried meal Bell tied him to one of the veranda posts, that he might not commit any act vicious enough to keep them at home. As he had a huge pocket full of apricots he was in perfect good-humor, not taking his confinement at all to heart, inasmuch as it commanded a full view of the scene of action. His amiability was further increased, moreover, by the possession of a bright new policeman's whistle, which was carefully tied to his button-hole by a neat little silk cord, and which his fond parents intended that he should blow if he chanced to fall into danger during his rambles about the camp. We might as well state here, however, that this precaution proved fruitless, for he blew it at all times and seasons; and everybody became so hardened to its melodious shriek that they paid no attention to it whatever, — history, or fable, thus again repeating itself.

Mr. and Mrs. Noble had driven Margery and Phil into town from the fruit ranch, and were waiting to see the party off.

Mrs. Oliver was to live in the Winship house during the absence of the family, and was aiding them to do those numberless little things that are always found undone at the last moment. She had given her impetuous daughter a dozen fond embraces, smothering in each a gentle warning, and stood now with Mrs. Winship at the gate, watching the three girls, who had gone on to bid Elsie good-by.

"I hope Pauline won't give you any trouble," she said. "She is so apt to be too impulsive and thoughtless."

"I shall enjoy her," said sweet aunt Truth, with that bright, cordial smile of hers that was like a blessing. "She has a very loving heart, and is easily led. How pretty the girls look, and how different they are! Polly is like a thistledown or a firefly, Margery like one of our home Mayflowers, and I can't help thinking my Bell like a sunbeam."

The girls did look very pretty; for their mothers had fashioned their camping-dresses with much care and taste, taking great pains to make them picturesque and appropriate to their summer life "under the greenwood tree."

Over a plain full skirt of heavy crimson
serge Bell wore a hunting jacket and drapery
of dark leaf-green, like a bit of forest against
a sunset. Her hair, which fell in a waving
mass of burnished brightness to her waist, was
caught by a silver arrow, and crowned by a wide
soft hat of crimson felt encircled with a bird's
breast.

Margery wore a soft gray flannel, the color
of a dove's throat, adorned with rows upon
rows of silver braid and sparkling silver but-
tons; while her big gray hat had nothing but
a silver cord and tassel tied round it in Spanish
fashion.

Polly was all in sailor blue, with a distractingly natty little double-breasted coat and great
white rolling collar. Her hat swung in her
hand, as usual, showing her boyish head of
sunny auburn curls, and she carried on a neat
chatelaine a silver cup and little clasp knife,
as was the custom in the party.

"It's very difficult," Polly often exclaimed,
"to get a dress that will tone down your hair
and a hat that will tone up your nose, when
the first is red and the last a snub! My nose
is the root of all evil; it makes people think
I'm saucy before I say a word; and as for my
hair, they think I must be peppery, no matter

if I were really as meek as Moses. Now there's Margery, the dear, darling mouse! People look at her two sleek braids, every hair doing just what it ought to do and lying straight and smooth, and ask, 'Who is that sweet girl?' There's something wrong somewhere. I ought not to suffer because of one small, simple, turned-up nose and a head of hair which reveals the glowing tints of autumn, as Jack gracefully says."

"Here they come!" shouted Jack from the group on the Howards' piazza. "Christopher Columbus, what gorgeousness! The Flamingo, the Dove, and the Blue-jay! Good morning, young ladies; may we be allowed to travel in the same steamer with your highnesses?"

"You need n't be troubled," laughed Bell. "We shall not disclose these glories until we reach the camp. But you are dressed as usual. What's the matter?"

"Why, the fact is," answered Geoffrey, "our courage failed us at the last moment. We donned our uniforms, and looked like brigands, highway robbers, cowboys, firemen,— anything but modest young men; and as it was too warm for ulsters, we took refuge in civilized raiment for to-day. When we arrive, you shall behold our dashing sombreros fixed up with peacock feathers, and our refulgent shirts, which are of the most original style and decoration."

"Aboriginal, in fact," said Jack. "We have broad belts of alligator skin, pouches, pistols, bowie-knives, and tan-colored shoes; but we dislike to flaunt them before the eyes of a city public."

"Here they are!" cried Geoffrey, from the gate. "Uncle, and aunt, and Dicky, and — good gracious! Is he really going to take that wretched tan terrier?"

"Won't go without him," said Bell, briefly. "There are cases where it is better to submit than to fight."

So the last good-bys were said, and Elsie bore up bravely; better, indeed, than the others, who shed many a furtive tear at leaving her. "Make haste and get well, darling," whispered the girls, lovingly.

"Pray, pray, dear Mrs. Howard, bring her down to us as soon as possible. We'll take such good care of her," teased Bell, with one last squeeze, and strong signs of a shower in both eyes.

"Come, girls and boys," said kind Dr. Paul, "the steamer has blown her first whistle, and we must be off."

Oh, how clear and beautiful a day it was, and how charmingly gracious Dame Ocean looked in her white caps and blue ruffles! Even the combination steamboat smell of dinner, oil, and close air was obliterated by the keen sea breeze.

The good ship Orizaba ploughed her way through the sparkling, sun-lit waves, traversing quickly the distance which lay between the young people and their destination. They watched the long white furrow that stretched in her wake, the cloud of black smoke which floated like a dark shadow above the laughing crests of the waves, and the flocks of sea-gulls sailing overhead, with wild shrill screams ever and anon swooping down for some bit of food flung from the ship, and then floating for miles on the waves.

How they sung "Life on the Ocean Wave," "Bounding Billow," and "Rocked in the Cradle of the Deep"! How Jack chanted, —

"I wish I were a fish,
     With a great long tail;
   A tiny little tittlebat,
     A wiggle or a whale,
In the middle of the great blue sea.   Oh, my!"

"Oh, how I long to be there!" exclaimed Philip, "to throw aside all the formal customs of a wicked world I abhor, and live a free life under the blue sky!"

"Why, Philip Noble! I never saw you inside of a house in my life," cried Polly.

"Oh, yes; you're mistaken. I've been obliged to eat most of my meals in the house, and sleep there; but I don't approve of it, and it's a trial to be borne with meekness only when there's no remedy for it."

"Besides," said Jack, "even when we are out-of-doors we are shelling the reluctant almond, poisoning the voracious gopher, pruning grape-vines, and 'sich.' Now I am only going to shoot to eat, and eat to shoot!"

"Hope you've improved since last year, or you'll have a low diet," murmured Phil, in an undertone.

"The man of genius must expect to be the butt of ridicule," sighed Jack, meekly.

"But you'll not repine, although your heart-strings break, will you?" said Polly, sympathizingly; "especially in the presence of several witnesses who have seen you handle a gun."

"How glad I am that I'm too near-sighted to shoot," said Geoffrey, taking off the eye-glasses that made him look so wise and dignified. "I shall lounge under the trees, read Macaulay, and order the meals."

" I shall need an assistant about the camp,"
said aunt Truth, smilingly; " but I hardly
think he 'll have much time to lounge; when
everything else fails, there 's always Dicky, you
know."

Geoffrey looked discouraged.

" And, furthermore, I declare by the nose of
the great Tam O'Shanter that I will cut down
every tree in the vicinity ere you shall lounge
under it," said Jack.

" Softly, my boy. Hill's blue gum forest is
not so very far away. You 'll have your hands
full," laughed Dr. Paul.

Here Margery and Bell joined the group,
after a quick walk up and down the deck.

" Papa," said Bell, excitedly, " we certainly
are nearing the place. Do you see that bend
in the shore, and don't you remember that the
landing is n't far below ? "

" Bell's bump of locality is immense. There
are nineteen bends in the shore exactly like
that one before we reach the landing. How
many knots an hour do you suppose this ship
travels, my fair cousin ? " asked Geoffrey.

" I could tell better," replied Bell, calmly,
" if I could ever remember how many knots
made a mile, or how many miles made a knot ;
but I always forget."

" Oh, see ! There 's a porpoise ! " cried Jack. " Polly, why is a porpoise like a water-lily ? "

But before he could say " Guess," Phil, Geoff, and the girls had drawn themselves into a line, and, with a whispered " One, two, three," to secure a good start, replied in concert, " We–give–it–up ! "

" What a deafening shout ! " cried aunt Truth, coming out of the cabin. " What 's the matter, pray ? "

" Nothing, aunty," laughed Polly. " But we have formed a society for suppressing Jack's conundrums, and this is our first public meeting. How do you like the watchword ? "

Aunt Truth smiled. " It was very audible," she said. " Yours is evidently not a secret society."

" I wish I could find out who originated this plan," quoth Jack, murderously. " But I suppose it 's one of you girls, and I can't revenge myself. Oh, when will this barrier between the sexes be removed ! "

" I trust not in your lifetime," shuddered Polly, " or we might as well begin to ' stand round our dying beds ' at once."

CHAPTER II.

THE JOURNEY.

"Away, away, from men and towns,
To the wild wood and the downs,
To the silent wilderness."

WHATEVER the distance was in reality, the steamer had consumed more time than usual, and it was quite two o'clock, instead of half past twelve, as they had expected, before they were landed on the old and almost forgotten pier, and saw the smoke of the Orizaba as she steamed away.

After counting over their bags and packages to see if anything had been forgotten, they looked about them.

There was a dirty little settlement, a mile or two to the south, consisting of a collection of tumble-down adobe houses, which looked like a blotch on the brown hillside; a few cattle were browsing near by, and the locality seemed to be well supplied with lizards, which darted over the dusty ground in all directions. But the startling point of the landscape was that it showed no sign of human life, and Pancho's orders had been to have Señor Don Manuel Felipe Hilario Noriega and his wood-cart on hand promptly at past half twelve.

" Can Pancho have forgotten ? "

" Can he have lost his way and never arrived here at all ? "

" Can Señor Don Manuel Felipe Hilario Noriega have grown tired of waiting and gone off ? "

" Has Señor Don Manuel Felipe Hilario Noriega been drinking too much aguardiente and so forgotten to come ? "

" Has Pancho been murdered by highway robbers, and served up into stew for their evening meal ? "

" With Hop Yet for dessert ! Oh, horrible ! "

These were some of the questions and exclamations that greeted the ears of the lizards, and caused them to fly over the ground in a more excited fashion than ever.

" One thing is certain. If Pancho has been stupid enough to lose his way coming fifty miles down the coast, I 'll discharge him," said Dr. Winship, with decision.

"When you find him," added aunt Truth, prudently.

"Of course. But really, mamma, this looks discouraging; I am afraid we can't get into camp this evening. Shall we go up to the nearest ranch house for the night, and see what can be done to-morrow?"

"Never!" exclaimed the young people, with one deafening shout.

"Never," echoed Philip separately. "I have vowed that a bed shall not know me for three months, and I'll keep my vow."

"What do you say to this, uncle Doc?" said Geoffrey. "Suppose you go up to the storehouse and office, — it's about a mile, — and see if the goods are there all right, and whether the men saw Pancho on his way up to the cañon. Meanwhile, Phil and I will ride over here somewhere to get a team, or look up Señor Don Manuel Felipe Hilario Noriega. Jack can stay with aunt Truth and the girls, to watch developments."

"But, papa, can't we pitch the camp to-night, somehow?" asked Bell, piteously.

"I don't see how. We are behindhand already; and if we get started within an hour we can't reach the ground I selected before dark; and we can't choose any nearer one, because if Pancho is anywhere in creation he is on the identical spot I sent him to."

"But, Dr. Paul, I'll tell you what we could do," suggested Jack. "If we get any kind of a start, we can't fail to reach camp by seven or eight o'clock at latest. Now it's bright moonlight, and if we find Pancho, he'll have the baggage unloaded, and Hop Yet will have a fire lighted. What's to prevent our swinging the hammocks for the ladies? And we'll just roll up in our blankets by the fire, for to-night. Then we'll get to housekeeping in the morning."

This plan received a most enthusiastic reception.

"Very well," replied the Doctor. "If you are all agreed, I suppose we may as well begin roughing it now as at any time."

You may have noticed sometimes, after having fortified yourself against a terrible misfortune which seemed in store for you, that it didn't come, after all. Well, it was so in this case; for just as Dr. Winship and the boys started out over the hillside at a brisk pace, an immense cloud of dust, some distance up the road, attracted their attention, and they came to a sudden standstill.

The girls held their breath in anxious expectation, and at length gave an irrepressible shout of joy and relief when there issued from the dense gray cloud the familiar four-horse team, with Daisy, Tule Molly, Villikins and Dinah, looking as fresh as if they had not been driven a mile, tough little mustangs that they were.

A long conversation in Spanish ensued, which, being translated by Dr. Winship, furnished all necessary information concerning the delay.

S. D. M. F. H. N. stated that Pancho was neither faithless nor stupid, but was waiting for them on the camping-ground, and that as the goods were already packed in his wood-cart he would follow them immediately. So the whole party started without more delay; Dr. and Mrs. Winship, Master Paul, Jack Howard, and the three girls riding in the wagon, while Geoffrey and Philip galloped ahead on horseback.

It was a long, dusty, tiresome ride; and Dicky, who had been as good all day as any saint ever carved in marble and set in a niche, grew rather warm, cross, and hungry, although he had been consuming ginger-snaps and apricots since early morning. After asking plaintively for the fiftieth time how long it would be before dinner, he finally succumbed to his weariness, and dropping his yellow head, that was like a cowslip ball, in his mother's lap, he fell asleep.

But the young people, whose eyes were not blinded by hunger and sleep, found more than enough to interest them on this dusty California road, winding as it did through grand old growths of trees, acres and acres of waving grain, and endless stretches of gorgeous yellow mustard, the stalks of which were five or six feet high, almost hiding from view the boys who dashed into the golden forest from time to time.

At the foot of the hill they passed an old adobe hut, with a crowd of pretty, swarthy, frowzy Mexican children playing in the sunshine, while their mother, black-haired and ample of figure, occupied herself in hanging great quantities of jerked beef on a sort of clothes-line running between the eucalyptustrees.

The father, a wild-looking individual in a red shirt and enormous hat, came from behind the hut, unhitched the stout little broncho tied to the fence, gave the poor animal a desperately tight " cinch," threw himself into the saddle without touching his foot to the lumbering wooden stirrups, and, digging his spurs well into the horse's sides, was out of sight in an instant, leaving only a huge cloud of dust to cover his disappearance.

"How those fellows do ride!" exclaimed Dr. Winship, savagely. "I wish they were all obliged to walk until they knew how to treat a horse."

"Then they'd walk straight into the millennium," said Jack sagely, "for their cruelty seems to be an instinct."

"But how beautifully they ride, too!" said Polly. "Mamma and I were sitting on the hotel piazza the other day, watching two young Spaniards who were performing feats of horsemanship. They dropped four-bit pieces on the dusty road, and riding up to them at full speed clutched them from the ground in some mysterious way that was perfectly wonderful. Then Nick Gutierrez mounted a bucking horse, and actually rolled and lighted a cigarette while the animal bucked with all his might."

"See that cunning, cunning *muchachita,* mamma!" cried Bell; for, as they stopped at the top of the hill to let the horses breathe, one of the little Mexican children ran after them, holding out a handful of glowing yellow poppies.

She was distractingly pretty, with a beauty that is short-lived with the people of her race. The afternoon sun shone down fiercely on her waving coal-black locks, and brought a rich color to her nut-brown cheek; she had one little flimsy, ragged garment, neither long, broad, nor thick, which hung about her picturesquely; and, with her soft, dark, sleepy eyes, the rows of little white teeth behind her laughing red mouth, and the vivid yellow blossoms in her tiny outstretched hand, she was a very charming vision.

"*Como te llamas, muchachita?*" (What is your name, little one?) asked Bell, airing her Spanish, which was rather good.

"Teresita," she answered, with a pretty accent, as she scratched a set of five grimy little toes to and fro in the dusty ground.

"Throw her a bit, papa," whispered Bell; and, as he did so, Teresita caught the piece of silver very deftly, and ran excitedly back to the centre of the chattering group in front of the house.

"How intense everything is in California! Do you know what I mean, mamma?" said Bell. "The fruit is so immense, the cañons so deep, the trees so big, the hills so high, the rain so wet, and the drought so dry."

"The fleas so many, the fleas so spry," chanted Jack, who had perceived that Bell was talking in rhyme without knowing it. "California is just the place for you, Bell; it gives you a chance for innumerable adjectives heaped one on the other."

"I don't always heap up adjectives," replied Bell, with dignity. "When I wish to describe you, for instance, I simply say 'that hateful boy,' and let it go at that."

Jack retired to private life for a season.

"I'd like to paint a picture of Teresita," said Margery, who had a pretty talent for sketching, "and call it The Summer Child, or some such thing. I should think the famous old color artists might have loved to paint this gorgeous flame-tinted poppy."

"Not poppy, — eschscholtzia," corrected Jack, coming rapidly to the surface again, after Bell's rebuke, and delivering himself of the tongue-confusing word with a terrible grimace.

"I'm not writing a botany," retorted Margery; "and I can never remember that word, much less spell it. I don't see how it grows under such an abominable Russian name. It's worse than ichthyosaurus. Do you remember that funny nonsense verse? —

"I is for ichthyosaurus,
   Who lived when the world was all porous ;
      But he fainted with shame
      When he first heard his name,
   And departed a long while before us."

" The Spaniards are more poetic," said aunt Truth, " for they call it *la copa de oro*, the golden cup. Oh, see them yonder ! It is like the Field of the Cloth of Gold."

The sight would have driven a royal florist mad with joy : a hillside that was a swaying mass of radiant bloom, a joyous carnival of vivid color, in which the thousand golden goblets, turned upward to the sun, were dancing, and glowing, and shaming out of countenance the purple and blue and pink masses which surrounded them on every side.

" You know Professor Pinnie told us that every well-informed young girl should know at least the flora of her own State," said Jack, after the excitement had subsided.

" Well, one thing is certain : Professor Pinnie never knew the *state* of his own *flora*, or at least he kept his wife sorting and arranging his specimens all the time ; and I think he 's a regular old frump," said Polly, irreverently, but meeting aunt Truth's reproving glance, which brought a blush and a whispered " Excuse me," she went on, " Well, what I mean is, he does n't know any more than other people, after all; for he cares for nothing but bushes and herbs and seeds and shrubs and roots and stamens and pistils; and he can't tell whether a flower is lovely or not, he is so crazy to find out where it belongs and tie a tag round it."

"I must agree with Polly," laughed Jack. "Why, I went to ride with him one day in the Cathedral Oaks, and he made me get off my horse every five minutes to dig up roots and tie them to the pommel of his old saddle, so that we came into town looking like moving herbariums. The stable-man lifted him on to his horse when he started, I suppose, and he would have been there yet if he had n't been helped off. Bah!" For Jack had a supreme contempt for any man who was less than a centaur.

By this time they had turned off the main thoroughfare, and were traveling over a bit of old stage road which was anything but easy riding. There they met some men who were driving an enormous band of sheep to a distant ranch for pasture, which gave saucy Polly the chance to ask Dr. Winship, innocently, why white sheep ate so much more than black ones.

He fell into the trap at once, and answered unsuspectingly, in a surprised tone, "Why, do they?" giving her the longed-for opportunity to respond, "Yes, of course, because there are so many more of 'em; don't you see?"

"You are behind the times, Dr. Paul," said Jack. "That's an ancient joke. Just look at those sheep, sir. How many are there? Eight hundred, say?"

"Even more, I should think, — a thousand, certainly; and rather thin they look, too."

"I should imagine they might," said Bell, sympathetically. "When I first came to California I never could see how the poor creatures found anything to eat on these bare brown hillsides, until the farmers showed me the prickly little burr clover balls that cover the ground. But see, mamma! there are some tiny lambs, poor tired, weak-legged little things; I wonder if they will live through the journey."

"Which reminds me," said Jack, giving Villikins a touch of the whip, "that nothing is so calculated to disturb your faith in and love for lambs as life on a sheep ranch. Innocent! Good gracious! I never saw such — such" —

"Gasping, staggering, stuttering, stammering tom-fools," interposed Bell. "That's what Carlyle called *one* Lamb, — dear Mr. 'Roast Pig' Charles; and a mean old thing he was, too, for doing it."

"Well, it is just strong enough to apply to the actual lamb; not the lamb of romance, but the lamb of reality. You can't get him anywhere; he does n't know enough. He won't drive, he can't follow; he's too stupid. Why, I went out for a couple of 'em once, that were lost in the cañon. I found them, — that was comparatively easy; but when I tried to get them home, I could n't. At last, after infinite trouble, I managed to drive them up on to the trail, which was so narrow there was but one thing for a rational creature to do, and that was to go ahead. Then, if you'll believe me, those idiots kept blaating and getting under the horse's fore-feet; finally, one of them, the champion simpleton, tumbled over into the cañon, and I tied the legs of the other one together, and carried him home on the front of my saddle."

"They are innocent, any way," insisted Margery. "I won't believe they're not. I can't bear these people who interfere with all your cherished ideas, and say that Columbus did n't discover America, and Shakespeare was n't Shakespeare, and William Tell did n't shoot the apple."

"Nevertheless, I claim that the lamb is not half so much an emblem of innocence as he is

of utter and profound stupidity. There is that
charming old lyric about Mary's little lamb; I
can explain that. After he came to school
(which was an error of judgment at the very
beginning), he made the rumpus, you know,

> " And then the teacher turned him out,
> But still he lingered nee-ar,
> And waited patiently about
> Till Mary did appee-ar.

Of course he did. He did n't know enough to
go home alone.

> " And then he ran to her and laid
> His head upon her arr-um,
> As if to say, ' I 'm not afraid ;
> You 'll keep me from all harr-um.'

As if a lamb could be capable of that amount
of reasoning ! And then

> " ' What makes the lamb love Mary so ? '
> The eager children cry ;
> 'Why, Mary loves the lamb, you know,'
> The teacher did reply.

And might have added that as Mary fed the
lamb three times a day and twice on Sundays,
he probably not only knew on which side his
daily bread was buttered, but also who buttered it."

"Dreadful boy!" laughed Bell. "Polly,
pray lower the umbrella; we are going to meet

some respectable people, and we actually are too dirty to be seen. I have really been eating dust."

"They must be equally dusty," said Polly, sagely. "Why, it is the Burtons, from Tacitas ranch!"

The Burton ranch wagon was drawn up, as its driver recognized Dr. Winship, and he proceeded to cheer the spirits of the party by telling them that he had passed Pancho two hours before, and that he was busily clearing rubbish from the camping-ground. This was six o'clock, and by a little after eight the weary, happy party were seated on saddle-blankets and carriage-cushions round a cheery camp-fire, eating a frugal meal, which tasted sweeter than nectar and ambrosia to their keen appetites.

The boys expressed their intention of spending the night in unpacking their baggage and getting to rights generally, but Dr. Winship placed a prompt and decisive veto on this proposition, and they submitted cheerfully to his better judgment.

Getting to bed was an exciting occupation for everybody. Dicky was first tucked up in a warm nest of rugs and blankets, under a tree, and sank into a profound slumber at once, with the happy unconsciousness of childhood. His father completed the preparations for his comfort by opening a huge umbrella and arranging it firmly over his head, so that no falling leaf might frighten him and no sudden gust of air blow upon his face.

Bell stood before her hammock, and meditated. " Well," she said, " going to bed is a simple matter, after all, when you have shorn it of all useless formalities. Let me see: I generally walk to and fro in the room, eating a bunch of grapes or an orange, look out of the window five or ten minutes, brush my hair, read my chapter in the Bible, take my book and study Spanish five minutes, on the principle of that abnormal woman who learned ninety-six languages while she was waiting for the kettle to boil in the morning " —

" Must have been a slow boiler," interrupted Polly, wickedly. " Seems to me it would have been economy to sell it and buy a new one."

" Oh, Polly! you are so willfully stupid! The kettle is n't the point — but the languages. Besides, she did n't learn all the ninety-six while the kettle was boiling once, you know."

" Oh, did n't she ? That alters the case. Thank you," said Polly, sarcastically.

"Now observe me," said Bell. "I have made the getting into a hammock a study. I first open it very wide at the top with both hands; then, holding it in that position, I gracefully revolve my body from left to right as upon an imaginary swivel; meantime I raise my right foot considerably from mother earth, with a view to passing it over the hammock's edge. Every move is calculated, you perceive, and produces its own share of the perfect result; the method is the same that Rachel used in rehearsing her wonderful tragic poses. I am now seated in the hammock, you observe, with both hands extending the net from side to side and the right foot well in position; I now raise the left foot with a swift but admirably steady movement, and I am — Help! Help!! Murder!!!"

"In short, you are not in, but out," cried Polly, in a burst of laughter; for Bell had leaned too far to the right, and on bringing the other foot in, with its "swift but admirably steady" motion, she gave a sudden lurch, pulled the hammock entirely over herself and fell out head first on the other side, leaving her feet tangled in its meshes. "Shall we help her out, Meg? She does n't deserve it, after that pompous oration and attempt to show off her superior abilities. Nevertheless, she always accepts mercy more gracefully than justice. Heave ahoy, my hearties!"

Bell was extricated, and looked sufficiently ashamed.

"We are much obliged for the lesson," said Margery, "but the method is open to criticism; so I think we'll manage in our ordinary savage way. We may not be graceful or scientific, but we get in, which is the main point."

The hammocks did not prove the easiest of nests, as the girls had imagined. In fact, to be perfectly candid about the matter, the wicked flea of California, which man pursueth but seldom catcheth, is apt, on many a summer night, to interfere shamelessly with slumber. On this particular night he was fairly rampant, perhaps because sweet humanity on which to feed was very scarce in that cañon.

"Good-night, girls!" called Jack, when matters seemed to be finally settled for sleep. "Bell, you must keep one eye open, for the coyotes will be stealing down the mountain in a jiffy, and yours is the first hammock in the path."

"Of course," moaned Bell, — "that's why the girls gave me this one; they knew very well that one victim always slakes the animals' thirst for blood. Well, let them come on. I shiver with terror, but my only hope is that I may be eaten in my sleep, if at all."

"There was a young party named Bell,
Who slept out-of-doors for a spell;
When asked how she fared,
She said she was scared,
But otherwise doing quite well.

"How's that?" asked Jack. "I shall be able to drive Bell off her own field, with a little practice."

"Go to sleep!" roared Dr. Paul. "In your present condition of mind and body you are not fit for poetry!"

"That's just the point, sir," retorted Jack, slyly, "for, you remember, poets are not *fit*, but *nascitur*,—don't you know?" and he retired under his blanket for protection.

But quiet seemed to be impossible: there were all sorts of strange sounds; and the moon, too, was so splendid that they almost felt as if they were lying beneath the radiance of a calcium light; while in the dark places, midst the branches of thick foliage, the owls hooted gloomily. If you had happened to be an owl in that vicinity, you might have heard not only the feverish tossing to and fro of the girls in the hammocks, but many dismal sighs and groans from Dr. Winship and the boys; for the bare ground is, after all, more rheumatic than romantic, and they too tumbled from side to side, seeking comfort.

But at midnight quiet slumber had descended upon them, and they presented a funny spectacle enough to one open-eyed watcher. A long slender sycamore log was extended before the fire, and constituted their pillow; on this their heads reposed, each decorated with a tightly fitting silk handkerchief; then came a compact, papoose-like roll of gray blanket, terminated by a pair of erect feet, whose generous proportions soared to different heights. There was a little snoring, too; perhaps the log was hollow.

At midnight you might have seen a quaintly despondent little figure, whose curly head issued from a hooded cloak, staggering hopelessly from a hammock, and seating herself on a mossy stump. From the limpness of her attitude and the pathetic expression of her eyes, I fear Polly was reviewing former happy nights spent on spring beds; and at this particular moment the realities of camping out hardly equaled her anticipations. Whatever may have been her feelings, however, they were promptly stifled when a certain insolent head reared itself from its blanket-roll, and a hoarse voice cackled, "Pretty Poll! Polly want a cañon?" At this insult, Miss Oliver wrapped her drapery about her and strode to her hammock with the air of a tragedy queen.

CHAPTER III.

LIFE IN THE CAÑON. — THE HEIR APPARENT LOSES HIMSELF.

"Know'st thou the land where the lemon-trees bloom,
    Where the gold orange glows in the green thicket's gloom;
    Where the wind, ever soft, from the blue heaven blows,
    And groves are of myrtle and olive, and rose?"

ON the next morning, as we have seen, they named their summer home Camp Chaparral, and for a week or more they were the very busiest colony of people under the sun; for it takes a deal of hard work and ingenuity to make a comfortable and beautiful dwelling-place in the forest.

The best way of showing you how they accomplished this is to describe the camp after it was nearly finished.

The two largest bedroom tents were made of

bright awning cloth, one of red and white, the other of blue and white, both gayly decorated with braid. They were pitched under the same giant oak, and yet were nearly forty feet apart; that of the girls having a canvas floor. They were not quite willing to sleep on the ground, so they had brought empty bed-sacks with them, and Pancho's first duty after his arrival had been to drive to a neighboring ranch for a great load of straw.

In a glorious tree near by was a " sky parlor," arranged by a few boards nailed high up in the leafy branches, and reached from below by a primitive ladder. This was the favorite sitting-room of the girls by day, and served for Pancho's bedroom at night. It was beautiful enough to be fit shelter for all the woodland nymphs, with its festoons of mistletoe and wild grape-vines; but Pancho was rather an unappreciative tenant, even going so far as to snore in the sacred place!

Just beyond was a card-room, — imagine it! — in which a square board, nailed on a low stump, served for a table, where Dr. Paul and the boys played many a game of crib, backgammon, and checkers. Here, too, all Elsie's letters were written and Bell's nonsense verses, and here was the identical spot where Jack

Howard, that mischievous knight of the brush, perpetrated those modern travesties on the " William Henry pictures," for Elsie's delectation.

The dressing-room was reached by a path cut through bushes to a charming little pool. Here were unmistakable evidences of feminine art : looking-glasses hanging to trees, snowy wash-cloths, each bearing its owner's initials, adorning the shrubs, while numerous towels waved in the breeze. Between two trees a thin board was nailed, which appeared to be used, as nearly as the woodpeckers could make out, as a toothbrush rack. In this, Philip, the skillful carpenter, had bored the necessary number of holes, and each one contained a toothbrush tied with a gorgeous ribbon.

In this secluded spot Bell was wont to marshal every morning the entire force of " the toothbrush brigade ; " and, conducting the drill with much ingenuity, she would take her victims through a long series of military manœuvres arranged for the toothbrush. Oh, the gaspings, the chokings and stranglings, which occurred when she mounted a rock by the edge of the pool, and after calling in tones of thunder,

" Brush, brothers, brush with care !
Brush in the presence of the commandaire ! "

ordered her unwilling privates to polish their
innocent molars to the tune of " Hail, Colum-
bia " or " Auld Lang Syne " ! And if they
became mutinous, it was Geoffrey who reduced
them to submission, and ordered them to brush
for three mornings to the tune of " Bluebells
of Scotland " as a sign of loyalty to their commander.

As for the furnishing of the camp, there
were impromptu stools and tables made of
packing-boxes and trunks, all covered with
bright Turkey red cotton ; there were no less
than three rustic lounges and two armchairs
made from manzanita branches, and a Queen
Anne bedstead was being slowly constructed,
day by day, by the ambitious boys for their
beloved Elsie.

One corner of each tent was curtained off
for a bath-room, another for a clothes-press,
and there were a dozen devices for comfort, as
Dr. Winship was opposed to any more incon-
venience than was strictly necessary. Dr. and
Mrs. Winship and little Dicky occupied one tent,
the boys another, and the girls a third.

When Bell, Polly, and Margery emerged
from their tent on the second morning, they
were disagreeably surprised to see a large
placard over the front entrance, bearing the

insolent inscription, " Tent Chatter." They
said nothing; but on the night after, a committee of two stole out and glued a companion
placard, " Tent Clatter," over the door of their
masculine neighbors. And to tell the truth, one
was as well deserved as the other; for if there
was generally a subdued hum of conversation
in the one, there never failed to be a perfect
din and uproar in the other.

Under a great sycamore-tree stood the
dining-table, which consisted of two long, wide
boards placed together upon a couple of bar-
rels; and not far away was the brush kitchen,
which should have been a work of art, for it
represented the combined genius of American,
Mexican, and Chinese carpenters, Dr. Winship,
Pancho, and Hop Yet having labored in its
erection. It really answered the purpose admirably, and looked quite like a conventional
California kitchen; that is, it was ten feet
square, and contained a table, a stove, and a
Chinaman.

The young people, by the way, had fought
bitterly against the stove, protesting with all
their might against taking it. Polly and Jack
declared that they would starve sooner than
eat anything that had n't been cooked over
a camp-fire. Bell and Philip said that they

should stand in front of it all the time, for
fear somebody would ride through the cañon
and catch them camping out with a *stove*.
Imagine such a situation; it made them blush.
Margery said she wished people were n't quite
so practical, and would n't ruin nature by
introducing such ugly and unnecessary things.
She intended to point the moral by drawing
a picture of Adam and Eve in the Garden
of Eden, — Eve bending over a cook-stove
and Adam peeling apples with a machine.
Geoffrey scoffed at Margery's sentimentalism,
put on his most trying air, and declared
that if he had his pork and onions served up
" hot and reg'lar," he did n't care how she had
her victuals cooked.

They were all somewhat appeased, however,
when they found that Dr. Winship was as anxious as they for an evening camp-fire, and
merely insisted upon the stove because it sim-
plified the cookery. Furthermore, being an
eminently just man, he yielded so far as to
give them permission to prepare their own
meals on a private camp-fire whenever they
desired; and this effectually stopped the argu-
ment, for no one was willing to pay so heavy
a price for effect.

The hammocks, made of gayly colored cords,

were slung in various directions a short distance from the square tent, which, being the
family sitting-room was the centre of attrac-
tion. It was arranged with a gay canopy, twenty
feet square. Three sides were made by hanging full curtains of awning cloth from redwood rods by means of huge brass rings.
These curtains were looped back during the
day and dropped after dark, making a cozy
and warm interior from which to watch the
camp-fire on cool evenings.

As for the Cañon de las Flores itself, this
little valley of the flowers, it was beautiful
enough in every part to inspire an artist's pencil or a poet's pen; so quiet and romantic it
was, too, it might almost have been under a
spell, — the home of some sleepy, enchanted
princess waiting the magic kiss of a princely
lover. It reached from the ocean to the mountains, and held a thousand different pictures on
which to feast the eye; for Dame Nature deals
out beauty with a lavish hand in this land of
perpetual summer, song, and sunshine. There
were many noble oak-trees, some hung pro-
fusely with mistletoe, and others with the long,
Spanish graybeard moss, that droops from the
branches in silvery lines, like water spray.
Sometimes, in the moonlight, it winds about

the oak like a shroud, and then again like a filmy bridal veil, or drippings of mist from a frozen tree.

Here and there were open tracts of ground between the clumps of trees, like that in which the tents were pitched, — sunny places, where the earth was warm and dry, and the lizards blinked sleepily under the stones.

Farther up the cañon were superb bay-trees, with their glossy leaves and aromatic odor, and the madroño, which, with its blood-red skin, is one of the most beautiful of California trees, having an open growth, like a maple, bright green lustrous leaves, and a brilliant red bark, which peels off at regular seasons, giving place to a new one of delicate pea-green.

There were no birches with pure white skin, or graceful elms, or fluffy pussy willows, but so many beautiful foreign things that it would seem ungrateful to mourn those left behind in the dear New England woods; and as for flowers, there are no yellow and purple violets, fragile anemones, or blushing Mayflowers, but in March the hillsides are covered with red, in April flushed with pink and blue, in May brilliant with yellow blossoms; and in the cañons, where the earth is moist, there are flowers all the year.

And then the girls would never forgive me
if I should forget the superb yucca, or Spanish bayonet, which is as beautiful as a tropical
queen. Its tall, slender stalk has no twigs or
branches, but its leaves hang down from the
top like bayonet-blades; and oh, there rises
from the centre of them such a stately princess
of a flower, like a tree in itself, laden with
cream-white, velvety, fragrant blossoms.

The boys often climbed the hillsides and
brought home these splendid treasures, which
were placed in pails of water at the tent doors,
to shed their luxuriant beauty and sweetness
in the air for days together. They brought
home quantities of Spanish moss, and wild
clematis, and manzanita berries too, with which
to decorate the beloved camp; and even Dicky
trotted back with his arms full of gorgeous
blossoms and grasses, which he arranged with
great taste and skill in mugs, bottles, and cans
on the dining-table.

Can't you see what a charming place it was?
And I have not begun to tell you the half yet;
for there was always a soft wind stirring the
leaves in dreamy music, and above and through
this whispered sound you heard the brook
splashing over its pebbly bed, — splashing and
splashing and laughing all it possibly could,

knowing it would speedily be dried up by the
thirsty August sun. Every few yards part of
the stream settled down contentedly into a
placid little pool, while the most inquisitive and
restless little drops flowed noisily down to see
what was going on below. The banks were
fringed with graceful alders and poison-oak
bushes, vivid in crimson and yellow leaves, while
delicate maiden-hair ferns grew in miniature
forests between the crevices of the rocks ; yet,
with the practicality of Chinese human nature,
Hop Yet used all this beauty for a dish-pan
and refrigerator !

Now, confess that, after having seen exactly
how it looks, you would like to rub a magic
lamp, like Aladdin, and wish yourself there
with our merry young sextette. For California
is a lovely land and a strange one, even at this
late day, when her character has been nearly
ruined by dreadful stories, or made ridiculous
by foolish ones.

When you were all babies in long clothes,
some people used to believe that there were
nuggets of gold to be picked up in the streets,
and that in the flowery valleys, flowing with
milk and honey, there grew groves of beet-
trees, and forests of cabbages, and shady bowers
of squash-vines ; and they thought that through

these fertile valleys strode men of curious mien, wild bandits and highway robbers, with red flannel shirts and many pockets filled with playing-cards and revolvers and bowie-knives; and that when you met these frightful persons and courteously asked the time of day, they were apt to turn and stab you to the heart by way of response.

Now, some of these things were true, and some were not, and some will never happen again; for the towns and cities no longer conduct themselves like headstrong young tomboys out on a lark, but have grown into ancient and decorous settlements some twenty-five or thirty years old.

Perhaps California is n't really so interesting since she began to learn manners; but she is a land of wonders still, with her sublime mountains and valleys; her precious metals; her vineyards and orchards of lemons and oranges, figs, limes, and nuts; her mammoth vegetables, each big enough for a newspaper story; her celebrated trees, on the stumps of which dancing-parties are given; her vultures; her grizzly bears; and her people, drawn from every nook and corner of the map, — pink, yellow, blue, red, and green countries. And though the story of California is not written, in all its romantic details, in the school-books of to-day, it is a part of the poetry of our late American history, full of strange and thrilling scenes, glowing with interest and dramatic fire.

I know a little girl who crossed the plains in that great ungeneraled army of fifteen or twenty thousand people that made the long and weary journey to the land of gold in 1849. She tells her children now of the strange, long days and months in the ox-team, passing through the heat and dust of alkali deserts, fording rivers, and toiling over steep mountains. She tells them how at night she often used to lie awake, curled up in her gray blanket, and hear the men talking together of the gold treasures they were to dig from the ground, — treasures, it seemed to her childish mind, more precious than those of which she read in "The Arabian Nights." And from a little hole in the canvas cover of the old emigrant wagon she used to see the tired fathers and brothers, worn and footsore from their hard day's tramp, some sleeping restlessly, and others guarding the cattle or watching for Indians, who were always expected, and often came ; and the last thing at night, when her eyes were heavy with sleep, she peered dreamily out into the darkness to see the hundreds of gleaming camp-fires, which dotted the plain as far as the eye could reach.

You will have noticed that this first week of camp-life was a quiet one, spent mostly by the young people in getting their open-air home comfortably arranged, making conveniences of all kinds, becoming acquainted with the cañon so far as they could, and riding once or twice to neighboring ranches for hay or provisions.

Dr. Winship believed in a good beginning; and, as this was not a week's holiday, but a summer campaign, he wanted his young people to get fully used to the situation before undertaking any of the exciting excursions in prospect. So, before the week was over, they began to enjoy sound, dreamless sleep on their hard straw beds, to eat the plain fare with decided relish, to grow a little hardy and brown, and quite strong and tough enough for a long tramp or horseback ride.

After a religious devotion to cold cream for a few nights, Polly had signified her terrible intention of "letting her nose go." "I disown it!" she cried, peeping in her tiny mirror, and lighting up her too rosy tints with a tallow candle. "Hideous objick, I defy thee! Spot and speckle, yea, burn to a crisp, and shed thy skin afterwards! I care not. Indeed, I shall be well rid of thee, thou — hm — thou — well, leopard, for instance."

One beautiful day followed another, each the exact counterpart of the one that had preceded it; for California boys and girls never have to say "wind and weather permitting" from March or April until November. They always know what the weather is going to do; and whether this is an advantage or not is a difficult matter to settle conclusively.

New England boys affirm that they would n't live in a country where it could n't rain any day it felt like it, and California lads retort that they are glad their dispositions are not ruined by the freaks of New England weather. At all events, it is a paradise for would-be campers, and any one who should assert the contrary would meet with energetic opposition from the loyal dwellers in Camp Chaparral.

Bell returned one day from a walk which she had taken by herself, while the other girls were off on some errand with the Doctor. After luncheon she drew them mysteriously into the square tent, and lowered the curtains.

"What is it?" Polly whispered, with an anxious expression of countenance. "Have you lost your gold thimble again, or your temper, or have you discovered a silver-mine?"

" I have found," she answered mysteriously, " the most beautifully secret place you ever beheld. It will be just the spot for us to write and study in when we want to be alone ; or it will even do for a theatre ; and it is scarcely more than half a mile up the cañon."

" How did you find it?" asked Margery.

" As I was walking along by the brookside, I saw a snake making its way through the bushes, and " —

" Goodness!" shrieked Polly, " I shall not write there, thank you."

" Goose! Just wait a minute. I looked at it, and followed at a distance ; it was a harmless little thing ; and I thought, for the fun of it, I would just push blindly on and see what I should find, because we are forever walking in the beaten path, and I long for something new."

" A bad instinct," remarked Madge, " and one which will get you into trouble, so you should crush it in its infancy."

" Well, I took up my dress and ploughed through the chaparral, until I came, in about three minutes of scratching and fighting, to an open circular place about as large as this tent.

It was exactly round, which is the curious part
of it; and in the centre was one stump, covered with moss and surrounded by great white
toadstools. How any one happened to go in
there and cut down a single tree I can't understand, nor yet how they managed to bring out
the tree through the tangled brush. It is so
strange that it seems as if there must be a
mystery about it."

"Certainly," said Margery promptly. "A
tragedy of the darkest kind! Some cruel
wretch has cut down, in the pride and pomp of
its beauty, one sycamore-tree; its innocent life-
blood has stained the ground and given birth
to the white toadstools which mark the spot
and testify to the purity of the victim."

"Well," continued Bell impressively, "I knew
I could never find it again; and I wanted so
much you should see it that I took the ball of
twine we always carry, unrolled it, and dropped
the thread all the way along to the brookside,
like Phrygia, or Melpomene, or Anemone, or
whatever her name was."

"Or Artesia, or Polynesia, or Euthanasia,"
interrupted Polly. "I think the lady you
mean is Ariadne."

"Exactly. Now we'll take papa to see it,
and then we'll fit it up as a retreat. Won't

it be charming? We'll call it the Lone
Stump."

"Oh, I like that; it makes me shiver!" cried
Polly. "I'm going to write an ode to it at
once. Ahem! It shall begin — let me see —

> "O lonely tree,
> What cruel 'he'
> Did lay thee low?
> Tell us the facts;
> Did cruel axe
> Abuse thee so?"

"Sublime! Second verse," said Bell slowly,
with pauses between the lines : —

> "Or did a gopher,
> The wicked loafer,
> Gnaw at thy base,
> And, doing so,
> Contrive to go,
> And leave no trace?"

"Oh dear!" sighed Margery; "if you will
do it, wait a minute.

> "O toadstools white,
> Pray give us light
> Upon the question.
> Did gopher gnaw,
> And live in awe
> Of indigestion?"

"Good!" continued Bell : —

> "Or did a man
> Malicious plan

The good tree's ruin,
And leave it so
Convenient low,
As seat for Bruin?

"For traveling grizzlies, you know. We may go there and see a hungry creature making a stump-speech, while an admiring audience of grasshoppers and tarantulas seat themselves in a circle on the toadstools."

"Charming prospect!" said Madge. "I don't think I care to visit the Lone Stump or pass my mornings there."

"Nonsense, dear child; it is just like every other part of the cañon, only a little more lonely. It is not half a mile from camp, and hardly a dozen steps from the place where the boys go so often to shoot quail."

"Very well," said the girls. "We must go there to-morrow morning; and perhaps we'd better not tell the boys, — they are so peculiar. Jack will certainly interfere with us in some way, if he hears about it."

"Now let us take our books and run down by the pool for an hour or two," said Bell. "Papa and the boys are all off shooting, and mamma is lying down. We can have a cool, quiet time; the sunshine is so hot here by the tents."

Accordingly, they departed, as they often did, for one of the prolonged chats in which school-girls are wont to indulge, and which so often, too, are but idle, senseless chatter.

These young people, however, had been fortunate in having the wisest and most loving guardianship, so that all their happy young lives had been spent to good purpose. They had not shirked study, and so their minds were stocked with useful information ; they had read carefully and digested thoroughly whatever they had read, so that they possessed a good deal of general knowledge. The girls were bright, sensible, industrious little women, who tried to be good, too, in the old-fashioned sense of the word ; and full of fun, nonsense, and chatter as they were among themselves, they never forgot to be modest and unassuming.

The boys were pretty well in earnest about life, too, with good ambitions and generous aspirations. They had all been studying with Dr. Winship for nearly two years ; and that means a great deal, for he was a real teacher, entering into the lives of his pupils, sympathizing with them in every way, and leading them, through the study of nature, of human beings, and of God, to see the beauty and meaning of life.

Geoffrey Strong, of course, was older than the rest, having completed his junior year at college; but Dr. Winship, who was his guardian, thought it wiser for him to rest a year and come to him in California, as his ambition and energy had already led him into greater exertions than his age or strength warranted. He was now studying medicine with the good Doctor, but would go back to the "land of perpetual pie" in the fall and complete his college course.

A splendid fellow he was, — so earnest, thoughtful, and wise; so gravely tender in all his ways to aunt Truth, who was the only mother he had ever known; so devoted to Dr. Winship, who loved him as his own elder son.

What will Geoffrey Strong be as a man? The twig is bent, and it is safe to predict how the tree will incline. His word will be as good as his bond; he will be a good physician, for his eye is quick to see suffering and his hand ready to relieve it; little children with feverish cheeks and tired eyes will love to clasp his cool, strong hand; he will be gentle as a woman, yet thoroughly manly, as he is now, for he has made the most of his golden youth, and every lad who does that will have a golden manhood and a glorious old age.

As for Philip Noble, he was a dear, good, trustworthy lad, too ; kindly, generous, practical, and industrious ; a trifle slow and reserved, perhaps, but full of common sense, — the kind of sense which, after all, is most uncommon.

Bell once said : " This is the difference between Philip and Geoffrey, — one does, and the other is. Geoff is the real simon-pure ideal which we praise Philip for trying to be," — a very good description for a little maiden whose bright eyes had only looked into life for sixteen summers.

And now we come to Jack Howard, who never kept still long enough for any one to write a description of him. To explain how he differed from Philip or Geoffrey would be like bringing the Equator and the Tropic of Cancer together for purposes of comparison.

If there were a horseback ride, Jack rode the wildest colt, was oftenest thrown and least often hurt ; if a fishing-party, Jack it was who caught all the fish, though he made more noise than any one else, and followed no rules laid down in The Complete Angler.

He was very often in trouble ;· but his misdemeanors were those of pure mischief, and were generally atoned for when it was possible. He excelled in all out-of-door sports. And indeed, if his prudence had at all kept pace with his ability, he might have done remarkable things in almost any direction; but he constantly overshot the mark, and people looked to him for the dazzling brilliancy and uncertainty of a meteor, but never for the steady glow of a fixed star.

Just now, Jack was a good deal sobered, and appeared at his very best. The teaching of Dr. Paul and the companionship of Geoffrey had done much for him, while the illness of his sister Elsie, who was the darling of his heart, acted constantly as a sort of curb upon him; for he loved her with all the ardor and passion which he gave to everything else. You might be fearful of Jack's high spirits and riotous mirth, of his reckless actions and heedless jokes, but you could scarcely keep from admiring the boy; for he was brave and handsome and winsome enough to charm the very birds off the bush, as aunt Truth acknowledged, after giving him a lecture for some misdemeanor.

The three girls made their way a short distance up the cañon to a place which they called Prospect Pool, because it was so entirely shut in from observation.

"Dear old Geoff!" said Bell, throwing her shawl over a rock and opening her volume of

Carlyle. "He has gone all through this for me, and written nice little remarks on the margin, — explanations and things, and interrogations where he thinks I won't know what is meant and had better find out, — bless his heart! What have you brought, Margery? By the way, you must move your seat away from that clump of poison-oak bushes; we can't afford to have any accidents which will interfere with our fun. We have all sorts of new remedies, but I prefer that the boys should experiment with them."

"It's the softest seat here, too," grumbled Margery. "We must get the boys to cut these bushes down. Why, you have n't any book, you lazy Polly. Are you going to sleep, or shall you chatter and prevent our reading?"

"Neither," she answered. "Here is a doughnut which I propose to send down the red pathway of fate; and here a pencil and paper with which I am going to begin our round-robin letter to Elsie."

"That's good! She has only had notes from Jack and one letter from us, which, if I remember right, had nothing in it."

"Thanks! I wrote it," sniffed Bell.

"Well, I meant it had no news, no account of things, you know."

"No, I would n't descend to writing news, and I leave accounts to the butcher."

"Stop quarreling, girls! This is my plan: I will begin in my usual rockety style, sometimes maliciously called the Pollyoliver method; Margery will take up the thread sedately; Bell will plunge in with a burst of enthusiasm and seventeen adjectives, followed by a verse of poor poetry; Geoff will do the sportive or instructive, just as he happens to feel; and Phil will wind up the letter by some practical details which will serve as a key to all the rest. Won't it be a box of literary bonbons for her to read in bed, poor darling! Let me see! I represent the cayenne lozenges, sharp but impressive; Margery will do for jujube paste, which I adore, — mild, pleasant, yielding, delicious."

"Sticky and insipid!" murmured Madge, plaintively.

"Not at all, my dear. Bell stands for the peppermints; Jack for chocolates, 'the ladies' delight;' Geoffrey for a wine-drop, altogether good, but sweetest in its heart; Phil — let me see! Phil is like — what is he like?"

"No more like candy than a cold boiled potato," said his sister.

"He is *candid*," suggested Bell. "Let us

call him rock-candy, pure, healthful, and far from soft."

"Or marshmallow," said Margery, "good, but tough."

"Or caramel," laughed Polly; "it always sticks to a point."

"Thanks, gentle creatures," said a voice from the bushes on the other side of the pool, and Phil stalked out from his covert, like a wounded deer.

"How long have you been in there, villain?" cried Bell.

"Ever since lunch; but I only waked from a sound sleep some twenty minutes ago. I've heard a most instructive conversation — never been more amused in my life; don't know whether I prefer being a cold boiled potato or a ladies'-delight!"

"You have n't any choice," snapped Polly, a trifle embarrassed at having been overheard.

"I'm glad it was my own sister who called me a c. b. p. (the most loathsome thing in existence, by the way), because sisters never appreciate their brothers."

"I did n't call you a c. b. p.," remonstrated Margery. "I said you were no more like candy than a c. b. p. There is a difference."

"Is there? My poor brain fails to grasp it. But never mind; I 'll forgive you."

"Listeners never hear good of themselves," sighed Polly.

"Are you writing a copy-book, Miss Oliver? I did n't want to listen; it was very painful to my feelings, but I was too sleepy to move."

"And now our afternoon is gone, and we have not read a word," sighed little Margery. "I never met two such chatterboxes as you and Polly."

"And to hear us talk is a liberal education," retorted Polly.

"Exactly," said Philip, dryly. "Come, I 'll take the books and shawls. It 's nearly five o'clock, and we shall hear Hop Yet blowing his lusty dinner-horn presently."

"Why did n't you go off shooting with the others?" asked Margery.

"Stayed at home so they 'd get a chance to shoot."

"Why, do you mean you always scare the game away?" inquired Polly, artlessly.

"No; I mean that I always do all the shooting, and the others get discouraged."

"Clasp hands over the bloody chasm," said Bell, "and let us smoke the pipe of peace at dinner."

Philip and Bell came through the trees, and, as they neared the camp, saw aunt Truth sitting at the door of Tent Chatter, looking the very picture of comfort, as she drew her darning-needle in and out of an unseemly rent in one of Dicky's stockings. Margery and Polly came up just behind, and dropped into her lap some beautiful branches of wild azalea.

"Did you have a pleasant walk, dears?" she asked.

"Yes, indeed, dear auntie. Now, just hold your head perfectly still, while we decorate you for dinner. We will make uncle Doc's eyes fairly pop with admiration. Have you been lonely without us?"

"Oh, not a bit. You see there has been a good deal of noise about here, and I felt as if I were not alone. Hop Yet has been pounding soap-root in the kitchen, and I hear the sound of Pancho's axe in the distance, — the Doctor asked him to chop wood for the camp-fire. Was Dicky any trouble? Where is he?"

"Why, darling mother, are you crazy?" asked Bell. "If you think a moment, he was in the hammock and you were lying down in the tent when we started."

"Why, I certainly thought I heard him ask to go with you," said Mrs. Winship, in rather an alarmed tone.

"So he did; but I told him it was too far."

"I did n't hear that; in fact, I was half asleep; I was not feeling well. Ask Hop Yet; he has been in the kitchen all the afternoon."

Hop Yet replied, with discouraging tranquillity, "Oh, I no know. I no sabe Dicky; he allee time lun loun camp; I no look; too muchee work. I chop hash — Dicky come in kitch' — make heap work — no good. I tell him go long — he go; bime-by you catchum; you see." Whereupon he gracefully skinned an onion, and burst into a Chinese song, with complete indifference as to whether Dicky lived or died.

"Perhaps he is with Pancho; I 'll run and see!" cried Polly, dashing swiftly in the direction of the sky-parlor. But after a few minutes she ran back, with a serious face. "He 's not there; Pancho has not seen him since lunch."

"Well, I 've just happened to think," said pale aunt Truth, "that papa came into the tent for some cartridges, after you left, and of course he took Dick with him. I don't suppose it is any use to worry. He always does come out right; and I have told him so many times never on any account to go away from the camp alone that he surely would not do it. Papa and the boys will be home soon, now. It is nearly six o'clock, and I told them that I would blow the horn at six, as usual. If they are too far away to hear it, they will know the time by the sun."

"Well," said Bell, anxiously, "I hope it is all right. Papa is so strict that he won't be late himself. Did all the boys go with him, mamma?"

"Yes, all but Philip."

"Oh, then Dicky must be with them," said Margery, consolingly. "Geoffrey always takes him wherever he can."

So the girls went into the tent to begin their dinner toilet, which consisted in carefully brushing burrs and dust from their pretty dresses, and donning fresh collars and stockings, with low ties of russet leather, which Polly declared belonged only to the stage conception of a camping costume; then, with smoothly brushed hair and bright flower-knots at collar and belt, they looked charming enough to grace any drawing-room in the land.

The horn was blown again at six o'clock, aunt Truth standing at the entrance of the path which led up the cañon, shading her anxious eyes from the light of the setting sun.

"Here they come!" she cried, joyously, as the welcome party appeared in sight, guns over shoulder, full game-bags, and Jack and Geoff with a few rabbits and quail hanging over their arms.

The girls rushed out of the tent. Bell took in the whole group with one swift glance, and then turned to her mother, who, like most mothers, believed the worst at once, and grew paler as she asked, —

" Papa, where is little Dick ? "

" Dick ! Why, my dear, he has not been out with us. What do you mean ? "

" Are you sure you did n't take him ? " faltered aunt Truth.

" Of course I am. Good heavens ! Does n't any one know where the child is ? " looking at the frightened group.

" You know, uncle," said Geoffrey, " we started out at three o'clock. I noticed Dicky playing with his blocks in our tent, and said good-by to him. Did you see him when you came back for the cartridges ? "

" Certainly I did ; he called me to look at his dog making believe go to sleep in the hammock."

" We girls went down to the pool soon after that," said Bell, tearfully. " He asked to go with us, and I told him it was too far, and that he 'd better stay with mamma, who would be all alone. He said Yes so sweetly I could n't

mistrust him. Oh, was it my fault, papa?
Please don't say it was!" and she burst into
a passion of sobs.

"No, no, my child, of course it was not.
Don't cry; we shall find him. Go and look
about the camp, Geoff, while we consider for a
minute what to do."

"If there is any fault, it is mine, for going
to sleep," said poor aunt Truth; "but I never
dreamed he would dare to wander off alone,
my poor little disobedient darling! What shall
we do?"

"Have you spoken to Pancho and Hop
Yet?" asked Phil.

"Yes; they have seen nothing."

Hop Yet just at this moment issued from
his kitchen with an immense platter of mutton-
stew and dumplings, which he deposited on the
table. On being questioned again, he answered
as before, with the greatest serenity, intimating
that Dicky would come home "heap bime-by"
when he got "plenty hungly." He seemed to
think a lost boy or two in a family rather a
trifle than otherwise, and wound up his unfeel-
ing remarks with the practical one, "Dinner
all leady; you no eat mutton, he get cold!
Misser Wins', I no find pickle; you catchum!"

"I don't believe he would care if we all died

right before his eyes," muttered Polly, angrily. "I should just like to see a Chinaman's heart once, and find out whether it was made of resin, or cuttle-fish, or what."

"Well," said Phil, as Dr. Winship came through the trees from the card-room, "we must start out this instant, and of course we can find him somehow, somewhere; he has n't been gone over two hours, and he could n't walk far, that 's certain. Now, uncle Doc, shall we all go different ways, and leave the girls here to see if he does n't turn up?"

"Oh, papa," cried Bell, "do not leave us at home! We can hunt as well as any one; we know every foot of the cañon. Let me go with Geoff, and we 'll follow the brook trail."

"Very well. Now, mamma, Pancho and I will go down to the main road, and you wait patiently here. Make all the noise you can, children; and the one who finds him must come back to the camp and blow the horn. Hop Yet, we go now; if Dicky comes back, you blow the horn yourself, will you?"

"All light, boss. You eat um dinner now; then go bime-by; mutton heap cold; you" —

"Dinner!" shouted Jack. "Confound your impudence! if you say dinner again, I 'll cut the queue off your stupid head."

"Good!" murmured Polly, giving a savage punch to her blue Tam O'Shanter cap.

"Jack, Jack!" remonstrated aunt Truth.

"I know, dear auntie; but the callous old heathen makes me so mad I can't contain myself. Come, Margery, let's be off. Get your shawl; and hurrah for the one who comes back to blow the horn first! I'll wager you ten to one I'll have Dick in auntie's lap inside the hour!" — at which aunt Truth's eyes brightened, and she began to take heart again. But as he tore past the brush kitchen and out into the woods, dragging Madge after him at a breathless pace, he shut his lips together rather grimly, saying, "I'd give five hundred dollars (s'posin' I had a cent) to see that youngster safe again."

"Tell me one thing, Jack," said Margery, her teeth chattering with nervousness: "are there any animals in this cañon that would attack him?"

"Oh, of course it is possible that a California lion or a wild-cat might come down to the brook to drink, — they have been killed hereabouts, — but I hardly believe it is likely; and neither do I believe they would be apt to hurt him, any way, for he would never attack them, you know. What I am afraid of is that he has tumbled over the rocks somewhere in climbing, or tangled himself up in the chaparral. He could n't have made off with a pistol, could he? He is up to all such tricks."

Presently the cañon began to echo with strange sounds, which I have no doubt sent the owls, birds, and rabbits into fits of terror; for the boys had whistles and pistols, while Polly had taken a tin pan and a hammer. She had gone with Phil out behind the thicket of manzanita bushes, and they both stood motionless, undecided where to go.

"Oh, Phil, I can't help it; I must cry, I am so frightened. Let me sit down a second. Yes, I know it 's an ant-hill, and I should n't care if it were a hornet's nest, — I deserve to be stung. What do you think I said to Margery this morning? That Dicky was a perfect little marplot, and spoiled all our fun, and I wished he were in the bottom of the Red Sea; and then I called him a k-k-k-ill-joy!" and Polly buried her head in her blue Tam, and cried a good, honest, old-fashioned cry.

"There, chirk up, poor little soul, and don't you fret over a careless speech, that meant nothing at all. I 've wished him in the Red Sea more than once, but I 'm blessed if I ever do it again. Come, let 's go over yonder, where we caught the young owl; Dicky may have wanted to try that little game again."

So they went on, calling, listening, then struggling on again, more anxious every moment, but not so thoroughly dazed as Bell, who had rocked her baby-brother in his cradle, and to whom he was the embodiment of every earthly grace, if not of every heavenly virtue.

" I might have known this would happen," she said, miserably. " He is so careless that, if we ever find him again, we must keep him tied to something."

" Take care of your steps, dear," said Geoff, " and munch this cracker, or you won't have strength enough to go on with me. I wish it were not getting so dark; the moment the sun gets behind these mountain-tops the light seems to vanish in an instant. Dick-y ! "

" Think of the poor darling out in this darkness, — hungry, frightened, and alone," sighed Bell. " It 's past his bed-time now. Oh, why did we ever come to stay in this horrible place ! "

" You must not blame the place, dear ; we thought it the happiest in the world this morning. Here we are by the upper pool, and the path stops. Which way had we better go ? "

" I 've been here before, to-day," said Bell ; " we might follow the trail I made. But where is my string ? Light a match, Geoff, please."

" What string? What do you mean? "

" Why, I found a beautiful spot this morning, and, fearing I should n't remember the way again, I took out my ball of twine and dropped a white line all the way back, like Ariadne; but I don't see it. Where can it have disappeared, — unless Jack or Phil took it to tease me? "

" Oh, no ; I 've been with them all day. Perhaps a snake has swallowed it. Come."

But a bright idea had popped into Bell's head. " I want to go that way, Geoff, dear ; it 's as good as any other, and there are flowers just the other side, in an open, sunny place ; perhaps he found them."

" All right ; let 's go ahead."

" The trouble is, I don't know which way to go. Here is the rock ; I remember it was a spotted one, with tall ferns growing beside it. Now I went — let me see — this way," and they both plunged into the thick brush.

" Bell, Bell, this is utter nonsense ! " cried Geoff. " No child could crawl through this tangle."

" Dicky could crawl through anything in this universe, if it was the wrong thing; he is n't afraid of beast, bird, or fish, and he positively enjoys getting scratched," said Bell.

Meanwhile, what had become of this small hero, and what was he doing ? He was last seen in the hammock, playing with the long-suffering terrier, Lubin, who was making believe go to sleep. It proved to be entirely a make-believe ; for at the first loosening of Dicky's strangling hold upon his throat he tumbled out of the hammock and darted into the woods. Dicky followed, but Lubin was fleet of foot, and it was a desperate and exciting race for full ten minutes.

At length, as Lubin heard his little master's gleeful laugh, he realized that his anger was a thing of the past ; consequently, he wheeled about and ran into Dicky's outstretched arms, licking his face and hands exuberantly in the joy of complete forgiveness.

By this time the voice of conscience in Dicky's soul — and it was a very, very still, small one on all occasions — was entirely silenced. He strayed into a sunny spot, and picked flowers enough to trim his little sailor hat, probably divining that this was what lost children in Sunday-school books always did, and it would be dishonorable not to keep up the superstition. Then he built a fine, strong dam of stones across the brook, wading to and fro without the bother of taking off his shoes and stockings, and filled his hat with rocks and sunk it to the bottom for a wharf, keeping his hat-band to tie an unhappy frog to a bit of bark, and setting him afloat as the captain of a slave-ship. When, at length, the struggling creature freed himself from his bonds and leaped into the pool, Dicky played that he was a drowning child, and threw Lubin into the water to rescue him.

In these merry antics the hours flew by unnoticed; he had never been happier in his life, and it flashed through his mind that if he were left entirely to himself he should always be good.

"Here I 've been a whole day offul good by my lone self; have n't said one notty word or did one notty fing, nor gotted scolded a singul wunst, did I, Lubin? I guess we better live here; bettent we, Lubin? And ven we wunt git stuck inter bed fur wettin' our feets little teenty mites of wet evry singul night all the livelong days, will we, Lubin?"

But this was a long period of reflection for Master Dicky, and he capered on, farther and farther, the water sozzling frightfully in his little copper-toed boots. At length he sat down on a stone to rest himself, and, glancing aimlessly about, his eyes fell on a white string, which he grasped with alacrity, pulling its end from beneath the stone on which he sat.

"Luby Winship, the anjulls gaved me this string fur ter make an offul splendid tight harness for you, little Luby; and you can drag big heavy stones; won't that be nice?"

Lubin looked doubtful, and wagged his tail dissentingly, as much as to say that his ideas of angel ministrations were a trifle different.

But there was no end to the string! How very, very curious! Dicky wound and wound and crept and crept along, until he was thoroughly tired but thoroughly determined to see it through; and Lubin, meanwhile, had seized the first convenient moment, after the mention of the harness, to retire to the camp.

At length, oh, joy! the tired and torn little man, following carefully the leading - string, issued from the scratching bushes into a clean, beautiful, round place, with a great restful-looking stump in the centre, and round its base a small forest of snowy toadstools. What could be a lovelier surprise! Dicky clapped his hands in glee as he looked at them, and thought of a little verse of poetry which Bell had taught him: —

> "Some fairy umbrellas came up to-day
> Under the elm-tree, just over the way,

And as we have had a shower of rain,
The reason they came is made very plain :
To-night is the woodland fairies' ball,
And drops from the elm-tree might on them fall,
So little umbrellas wait for them here,
And under their shelter they 'll dance without fear.
Take care where you step, nor crush them, I pray,
For fear you will frighten the fairies away."

"Oh !" thought Dicky, in a trance of delight, "now I shall go to the fairies' ball, and see 'em dance under the cunning little teenty umberells ; and wunt they be mad at home when nobuddy can't see 'em but just only me ! And then if that potry is a big whopper, like that there uvver one, — 'laddin-lamp story of Bell's, — I 'll just pick evry white toadstool for my papa's Sunday dinner, and she sha'n't never see a singul fairy dance."

But he waited very patiently for a long, long time that seemed like years, for Lubin had disappeared ; and all at once it grew so dark in this thickly wooded place that Dicky's courage oozed out in a single moment, without any previous warnings as to its intention. The toadstools looked like the ghosts of little past-and-gone fairy umbrellas in the darkness, and not a single fairy couple came to waltz under their snowy canopies, or exchange a furtive kiss beneath their friendly shadows.

Dicky thought the situation exceedingly gloomy, and, without knowing it, followed the example of many older people, who, on being deserted by man, experience their first desire to find favor with God. He was not in the least degree a saintly child, but he felt instinctively that this was the proper time for prayer; and not knowing anything appropriate to the occasion, he repeated over and over again the time-worn plaint of childhood : —

> "Now I lay me down to sleep,
>   I pray the Lord my soul to keep ;
>   If I should die before I wake,
>   I pray the Lord my soul to take.   Amen."

Like older mortals of feeble faith, he looked for an immediate and practical answer, in the shape, perhaps, of his mother, with his little night-gown and bowl of bread and milk.

"My sakes alive!" he grumbled between his sobs, "they're the meanest fings I ever saw. How long do they s'pose I'm goin' to wait for 'em in this dark? When the bears have et me up in teenty snips, then they'll be saterfied, I guess, and wisht they'd tookened gooder care of me, — a little speck of a boy, lefted out in this dark, bear-y place, all by his lone self. O–oo–oo–oh!" and he wound up with a murderous yell, which had never failed before to bring the whole family to his side.

His former prayer seeming to be in vain, he found a soft place, brushed it as clean as possible, and with difficulty bending his little stiff, scratched body into a kneeling position, he prayed his nightly postscript to " Now I lay me : " " God bless papa, 'n' mamma, 'n' Bell, 'n' Jack, 'n' Madge, 'n' Polly, 'n' Phil, 'n' Geoff, 'n' Elsie." Then, realizing that he was in a perilous position, and it behooved him to be as pious as possible, he added : " And please bless Pancho, 'n' Hop Yet, 'n' Lubin, 'n' the goat, — not the wild goat up on the hill, but my goat, what got sick to his stummick when I painted him with black letters."

What a dreadful calamity, to be sure, if the wrong goat had been blessed by mistake ! His whole duty performed, he picked the toadstools for his papa's Sunday dinner, and, leaning his head against the lone stump, cried himself to sleep.

But relief was near, though he little suspected it as he lay in the sound, dreamless sleep which comes only to the truly good. There was a crashing sound in the still darkness, and Bell plunged through the thick underbrush with a cry of delight.

" He is here ! Dear, dear Geoff, he is all here ! I knew it, I knew it ! Hurrah ! — no,

I mean, Thank God!" she said softly, as she stooped down to kiss her mischievous little brother.

"But what a looking creature!" exclaimed Geoff, as he stooped over the recovered treasure. "See, Bell, his curls are glistening with pitch, his dress is torn into ribbons, and his hands — ugh, how dirty!"

"Poor little darling, he is thoroughly used up," whispered Bell, wiping tears of joy from her brown eyes. "Now I 'll run home like lightning, to blow the horn; and you carry Dicky, for he is too sleepy and stiff to walk; and, Geoff" (here she laid an embarrassed hand on his shoulder), "I 'm afraid he 'll be awfully cross, but you 'll not mind it, will you? He 's so worn out."

"Not I," laughed Geoff, as he dropped a brotherly kiss on Bell's pale cheek. "But I 've no idea of letting you go alone; you 're tired to death, and you 'll miss the path. I wish I could carry you both."

"Tired — afraid!" cried Bell, with a ringing laugh, while Dicky woke with a stare, and nestled on Geoffrey's shoulder as if nothing had happened. "Why, now that this weight is lifted off my heart, I could see a path in an untraveled forest! Good-by, you dear, darling, cruel boy! I must run, for every moment is precious to mamma." And with one strangling hug, which made Dicky's ribs crack, she dashed off.

Oh, how joyously, how sweetly and tunefully, the furious blast of the old cracked dinner-horn fell on the anxious ears in that cañon! It seemed clearer and more musical than a chime of silver bells.

In a trice the wandering couples had gathered jubilantly round the camp-fire, all embracing Bell, who was the heroine of the hour, — entirely by chance, and not through superior vision or courage, as she confessed.

It was hardly fifteen minutes when Geoff strode into the ring with his sorry-looking burden, which he laid immediately in aunt Truth's lap.

"Oh, my darling!" she cried, embracing him fondly, "to think you are really not dead, after all!"

"No, he is about as alive as any chap I ever saw." And while the happy parents caressed their restored darling, Geoff gathered the girls and boys around the dinner-table, and repeated some of Dicky's remarks on the homeward trip.

It seems that he considered himself the injured party, and with great ingenuity laid all the blame of the mishap on his elders.

"Nobuddy takes care of me, anyhow," he grumbled. "If my papa was n't a mean fing I 'd orter to have a black nurse with a white cap and apurn, like Billy Thomas, 'n' then I could n't git losted so offul easy. An' you all never cared a cent about it, either, or you 'd a founded me quicker 'n this — 'n' I 've been hungry fur nineteen hours, 'n' I guess I 've been gone till December, by the feelin', but you was too lazy to found me 'f I freezed to def — 'n' there ain't but one singul boy of me round the whole camp, 'n' 't would serveded you right if I had got losted forever ; then I bet you would n't had much fun Fourth of July 'thout my two bits 'n' my fire-crackers ! "

It was an hour or two before peace and quiet were restored to the camp. The long-delayed dinner had to be eaten ; and to Hop Yet's calm delight, it was a very bad one. Dicky's small wounds were dressed with sweet oil, and after being fed and bathed he was tucked lovingly into bed, with a hundred kisses or more from the whole party.

A little rest and attention had entirely restored his good-humor ; and when Dr. Paul went into the tent to see that all was safe for the night, he found him sitting up in bed with a gleeful countenance, prattling like a little angel.

"We had an offul funny time 'bout my gittin' losted, did n't we, mamma?" chuckled he, with his gurgling little laugh. "Next time I 'm goin' to get losted in annover bran'-new place where no-bud-dy can find me! I fink it was the nicest time 'cept Fourth of July, don't you, mamma?" And he patted his mother's cheek and imprinted an oily kiss thereon.

"Truth," said the Doctor, with mild severity, "I know you don't believe in applying the slipper, but I do think we should arrange some plan for giving that child an idea of the solemnity of life. So far as I can judge, he looks at it as one prolonged picnic."

"My sentiments, exactly!" cried Bell, energetically. "I can't stand many more of these trying scenes; I am worn to a ' shadder.' "

Dicky tucked his head under his mother's arm, with a sigh of relief that there was one person, at least, whose sentiments were always favorable and always to be relied upon.

"I love you the best of anybuddy, mamma," whispered he, and fell asleep.

CHAPTER IV.

RHYME AND REASON.

A BUDGET OF LETTERS FROM THE CAMP MAIL-BAG.

"The letter of a friend is a likeness passing true."

OUR friend Polly was seated in a secluded spot whence all but her had fled; her grave demeanor, her discarded sun-bonnet, her corrugated brow, all bespoke more than common fixedness of purpose, the cause of which will be discovered in what follows.

I. FROM THE COUNTESS PAULINA OLIVERA TO HER
FRIEND AND CONFIDANTE, THE LADY ELSIE HOWARD.*

*Scene : A sequestered nook in the Valley of the
Flowers.*

CAMP CHAPARRAL, *July* 6, 188–.

The countess is discovered at her ommerlu [1]
writing-table.   A light zephyr [2] plays with her
golden locks [3] and caresses her Grecian [4] nose, —
a nose that carries on its surface a few trifling
freckles, which serve but to call attention to its
exquisite purity of outline and the height of
its ambition.   Her eyes reflect the changing
shadows of moonlight, and her mouth is one
fit for sweet sounds; [5] yet this only gives you
a faint idea of the beauteous creature whose
fortunes we shall follow in our next number. [6]

I have given that style a fair trial, my dear
darling, but I cannot stand it another minute,
not being familiar with the language of what
our cook used to call the " fuddal aristocracy "
(feudal, you know).

I, your faithful Polly, am seated in the card-
room, writing with a dreadful pen which Phil

* Foot-notes by a rival of the Countess.
[1] Is that spelled right ?   [2] Fifty miles an hour, Jack says.
[3] Poetic license.   [4] Gone back to cold cream.
[5] And pie.   [6] For sale at all bookstores, ten cents a copy.

gave me yesterday. Its internal organs are filled with ink, which it disgorges when *pressed* to do so, but just now it is "too full for utterance," as you will see by the blots.

We have decided not to make this a real round-robin letter, like the last, because we want to write what we like, and not have it read by the person who comes next.

I have been badgered to death over my part of the communication sent to you last week, for the young persons connected with this camp have a faculty of making mountains out of mole-hills, as you know, and I have to suffer for every careless little speech. However, as we did n't wish to bore you with six duplicate letters, we invented a plan for keeping off each other's ground, and appointed Geoff a committee of one to settle our line of march. It is to be a collective letter, made up of individual notes; and these are Geoff's sealed orders, which must be obeyed, on pain of dismissal from the camp : —

No. 1 (Polly) is to amuse !
No. 2 (Phil)   "   inform.
No. 3 (Geoff)   "   edify ! !
No. 4 (Madge) "   gossip.
No. 5 (Bell)   "   versify.
No. 6 (Jack)   "   illustrate.

So, my dear, if you get any " information " or happen to be " edified " by what I write, don't mention it for worlds! (I just screamed my fears about this matter to Jack, and he says " I need n't fret." I shall certainly slap that boy before the summer is over.)

I could just tell you a lovely story about Dicky's getting lost in the woods the day before yesterday, and our terrible fright about him, and how we all joined in the boy-hunt, until Geoff and Bell found him at the Lone Stump ; but I suppose the chronicle belongs to Phil's province, so I desist. But what can I say ? Suppose I tell you that uncle Doc and the boys have been shooting innocent, *tame* sheep, skinning and cutting them up on the way home, and making us believe for two days that we were eating venison ; and we never should have discovered the imposition, had not Dicky dragged home four sheep-skins from the upper pool, and told us that he saw the boys "*peeling them off of a venison.*" Perhaps Phil may call this information, and Margery will vow that it is gossip and belongs to her ; any way, they consider it a splendid joke, and chuckle themselves to sleep over it every night ; but I think the whole affair is perfectly mad-dening, and it makes me boil with rage to be taken in so easily. Such a to-do as they make over the matter you never saw; you would think it was the first successful joke since the Deluge. (That was n't a *dry* joke, was it? Ha, ha!)

This is the way they twang on their harp of a thousand strings. At breakfast, this morning, when Jack passed me the corn-bread, I said innocently, "Why, what have we here?" "It is manna that fell in the night," answered Jack, with an exasperating snicker. "You did n't know mutton, but I thought, being a Sunday-school teacher, you would know something about manna." (N. B. He alludes to that time I took the infant class for Miss Jones, and they all ran out to see a military funeral procession.) "I wish you knew something about manners," snapped I; and then aunt Truth had to warn us both, as usual. Oh, dear! it 's a weary world. I 'd just like to get Jack at a disadvantage once!

~~We climbed Pico Negro yesterday. Bell, Geoff, Phil, and I had quite an experience in losing the trail. I will tell you about it. Just as ——~~

(Goodness me! what have I written? Oh, Elsie, pray excuse those *horizontal evidences* of my forgetfulness and disobedience. I have bumped my head against the table three times, as penance, and will now try to turn my thoughts into right channels. This letter is a black-and-white evidence that I have not a frivolous order of mind, and have always been misunderstood from my birth up to this date.)

We have had beautiful weather since — But no, of course Phil will tell you about the weather, for that is scarcely an amusing topic. I do want to be as prudent as possible, for uncle Doc is going to read all the letters (not, of course, aloud) and see whether we have fulfilled our specific obligations.

(I just asked Bell whether " specific " had a " c " or an " s " in the middle, and she answered " ' c,' of course," with such an air, you should have heard her! I had to remind her of the time she spelled "Tophet" with an " f " in the middle; then she subsided.)

(I just read this last paragraph to Madge, to see if she called it gossip, as I was going to take it out if it belonged to her topic, but she said No, she did n't call it gossip at all, — that she should call it slander!)

You don't know how we all long to see you, dear darling that you are. We live in the hope of having you with us very soon, and meanwhile the beautiful bedstead is almost finished, and a perfect success. (I wish to with-draw the last three quarters of that sentence, for obvious reasons ! !)

Dear, dear ! Geoffrey calls " Time up," and I 've scarcely said anything I should. Never, never again will I submit to this method of correspondence ; it is absolutely petrifying to one's genius. When I am once forced to walk in a path, nothing but the whole out-of-doors will satisfy me.

I 'm very much afraid I have n't amused you, dear, —

> But when I lie in the green kirk-yard,
> With the mould upon my breast,
> Say not that " she did well or ill,"
> Only, " She did her best."

Now, do you think that will interfere with Bell, when it 's only a quotation ? Any way, it 's so appropriate that uncle Doc will never have the heart to strike it out. The trouble is that Geoff thinks all the poetry in the universe is locked up in Bell's head, and if she once allows it to escape, Felicia Hemans and the rest will be too discouraged ever to try again ! (I can't remember whether F. H. is alive or not, and am afraid to ask, but you will know that I don't mean to be disrespectful.)

Laura, Anne, and Scott Burton were here

for the play, and Laura is coming down again
to spend the week. I can't abide her, and
there will probably be trouble in the camp.

The flame of my genius blazes high just
now, but Geoff has spoken, and it must be
snuffed. So good-by!

    Sizz-z-z!! and I'm *out!*

                 POLLIOLIVER.

II. FROM PHILIP TO ELSIE.

           CAMP CHAPARRAL, *July* 8, 188–.

MY DEAR ELSIE, — I believe I am to inform you concerning the daily doings of our
party, not on any account, however, permitting
myself to degenerate into "gossip" or "frivolous amusement."

They evidently consider me a quiet, stupid
fellow, who will fulfill such a task with no
special feeling of repression, and I dare say
they are quite right.

They call me the "solid man" of the camp,
which may not be very high praise, to be sure,
as Geoffrey carries his head in the clouds, and
Jack is — well, Jack is Jack! So, as the light
of a tallow dip is valuable in the absence of
sun and moon, I am raised to a fictitious reputation.

We fellows have had very little play so far,

for the furnishing of the camp has proved an immense undertaking, although we have plenty of the right sort of wood and excellent tools.

We think the work will pay, however, as Dr. Paul has about decided to stay until October, or until the first rain. He writes two or three hours a day, and thinks that he gets on with his book better here than at home. As for the rest of us, when we get fairly to rights we shall have regular study hours and lose no time in preparing for the examinations.

I suppose you know that you have a full bed-room set in process of construction. I say "suppose you know," because it is a profound secret, and the girls could never have kept it to themselves as long as this.

The lounging-chair is my allotted portion, and although it is a complicated bit of work, I accepted it gladly, feeling sure that you would use it oftener than any of the other pieces of furniture. I shall make it so deliciously easy that you will make me "Knight of the Chair," and perhaps permit me to play a sort of devoted John Brown to your Victoria. You will need one dull and prosy squire to arrange your pillows, so that you can laugh at Jack's jokes without weariness, and doze quietly while Geoff and uncle Doc are talking medicine.

Of course the most exciting event of the week was the mysterious disappearance and subsequent restoration of the Heir Apparent; but I feel sure somebody else will describe the event, because it is uppermost in all our minds.

Bell, for instance, would dress it up in fine style. She is no historian, but in poetry and fiction none of us can touch her; though, by the way, Polly's abilities in that direction are a good deal underrated. It 's as good as a play to get her after Jack when he is in one of his teasing moods. They are like flint and steel, and if aunt Truth did n't separate them the sparks would fly. With a girl like Polly, you have either to lie awake nights, thinking how you 'll get the better of her, or else put on a demeanor of gentleness and patience, which serves as a sort of lightning-rod round which the fire of her fun will play all day and never strike. Polly is a good deal of a girl. She seems at first to have a pretty sharp tongue, but I tell you she has a heart in which there is swimming-room for everybody. This may not be " information " to you, whom we look upon as our clairvoyant, but it would be news to most people.

Uncle Doc, Bell, Geoff, Polly, Meg, and I started for the top of Pico Negro the other morning. Bell rode Villikins, and Polly took a mule, because she thought the animal would be especially sure-footed. He was; in fact, he was so sure-footed that he did n't care to move at all, and we had to take turns in beating him up to the top. We boys walked for exercise, which we got to our heart's content.

It is only five or six miles from the old Mountain Mill (a picture of which Jack will send you), and the ascent is pretty stiff climbing, though nothing terrific. We lost the trail once, and floundered about in the chaparral for half an hour, till Bell began to make a poem on the occasion, when we became desperate, and dashed through a thicket of brush, tearing ourselves to bits, but stumbling on the trail at last. The view from the top is simply superb ! The valleys below are all yellow with grain-fields and green with vineyards, with here and there the roofs of a straggling little settlement. The depression in the side of the mountain (you will observe it in the picture) Polly says has evidently been " bitten out " by a prehistoric animal, and it turns out to be the loveliest little cañon imaginable.

We have had one novel experience, — that of seeing a tarantula-fight; and not between two, but five, tarantulas. We were about

twenty miles from camp, loping along a stretch
of hot, dusty road. Jack got off to cinch his
saddle, and so we all stopped a moment to let
our horses breathe. As I was looking about,
at nothing in particular, I noticed a black ball
in the deep dust at the side of the road. It
suddenly rolled over on itself, and I called to
the boys to watch the fun. We got off, hitched
our horses, and approached cautiously, for I
had seen a battle of the same kind before.
There they were, — five huge, hairy, dirty, black
creatures, as large as the palm of Dicky's
hand, all locked in deadly combat. They
writhed and struggled and embraced, their
long, curling legs fastening on each other with
a sound that was actually like the cracking of
bones. It takes a little courage to stand and
watch such a proceeding, for you feel as if
the hideous fellows might turn and jump for
you ; but they were doubtless absorbed in their
own battle, and we wanted to see the affair to
the end, so we took the risk, if there was any.
At last they showed signs of weariness, but we
prodded them up with our riding-whips, pre-
ferring that they should kill each other, rather
than do the thing ourselves. Finally, four of
them lay in the dust, doubled up and harmless, slain, I suppose, by their own poison. One,

the conquering hero, remained, and we dexterously scooped him into a tomato-can that Jack had tied to his saddle for a drinking-cup, covered him up with a handkerchief, and drew lots as to who should carry him home to Dr. Paul.

Knowing that the little beasts were gregarious, we hunted about for a nest, which we might send to you after ousting its disagreeable occupant. After much searching, we found a group of them, — quite a tarantula village, in fact. Their wonderful little houses are closed on the outside by a circular, many-webbed mesh, two or three inches across, and this web betrays the spider's den to the person who knows the tricks of the trade. Directly underneath it you come upon the tiny circular trap-door, which you will notice in the nest we send with these letters. You will see how wonderfully it is made, with its silken weaving inside, and its bits of bark and leaves outside ; and I know you will admire the hinge, which the tarantula must have invented, and which is as pretty a bit of workmanship as the most accomplished mechanic could turn out. We tore away the web and the door from one of the nests, and then poured water down the hole. The spider was at home, came out as fast as his clumsy legs would carry him, and clutched the end of the stick Jack held out to him. Then we tumbled him into the tomato-can just as he appeared to be making for us. The two didn't agree at all. One of them dispatched the other on the way home, — the same hero who had killed the other four; but, on hearing his bloody record, aunt Truth refused to have him about the camp; so we gave him an alcohol bath, and you shall see his lordship when you come. As Dr. Paul says they have been known to clear fourteen feet at a jump, perhaps you will feel happier to know that he is in alcohol, though their bite is not necessarily fatal if it is rightly cared for.

The girls have been patronizing the landscape by naming every peak, valley, grove, and stream in the vicinity; and as there is nobody to object, the names may hold.

We carry about with us a collection of strong, flat stakes, which have various names painted on them in neat black letters. Jack likes that kind of work, and spends most of his time at it; for now that Dr. Paul has bought a hundred acres up here, we are all greatly interested in its improvement.

Geoff has named the mountain Pico Negro, as I told you, and the little cañon on its side is called The Giant's Yawn. Then we have —

Mirror Pool,

The Lone Stump,

Field of the Cloth-of-Gold,

Cosy Nook,

The Imp's Wash-Bowl,

Dunce-Cap Hill,

The Saint's Rest, and

Il Penseroso Fall (in honor of Dicky, who was nearly drowned there).

If anybody fails to call these localities by their proper names he has to pay a fine of five cents, which goes towards beautifying the place. Dr. Paul has had to pay two fines for Bell, three for aunt Truth, and seven for Dicky; so he considers it an ill-judged arrangement.

Our encampment is supposed to be in the Forest of Arden, and Jack has begun nailing verses of poetry on the trees, like a second Orlando, save that they are not love poems at all, but appropriate quotations from Wordsworth or Bryant. And this brings me to our thrilling rendition of the play " As You Like It," last evening; but it is deserving of more than the passing notice which I can give it here.

One thing, however, I must tell you, as the girls will not write it of themselves, — that, although Bell carried off first honors and fairly captivated the actors as well as the audience, all three of them looked bewitching and acted with the greatest spirit, much better than we fellows did.

Of course we did n't give the entire play, and we had to "double up" on some of the characters in the most ridiculous fashion; but the Burtons helped out wonderfully, Scott playing Oliver, and Laura doing Audrey. They were so delighted with the camp that aunt Truth has invited them to come again on Saturday and stay a week.

At the risk of being called conceited I will also state that we boys consider that the stage management was a triumph of inventive art; we worked like beavers for two days and the results were marvelous, "if I do say so as should n't."

Just consider : we were "six miles from a lemon," as Sydney Smith would say, and yet we transformed all out of doors, first into an elegant interior, and then into a conventional stage forest.

A great deal of work is available for other performances, and so we do not regret it a bit; we propose doing "As You Like It" again when you are down here, and meanwhile we give diversified entertainments which Jack calls variety shows, but which in reality are very chaste and elegant occasions.

The other night we had a minstrel show, wearing masks of black cambric, with red mouths painted on them; you should have seen us, all in a dusky semicircle, seated on boards supported by nail-kegs: it was a scene better imagined than described. This is certainly the ideal way to live in summer time, and we should be perfectly happy and content if you could only shake off your troublesome cough and come to share our pleasure. We feel incomplete without you; and no matter how large our party may grow as the summer progresses, there will always be a vacant niche that none can fill save the dear little Saint who is always enshrined therein by all her loyal worshipers, and by none more reverently than her friend,

PHILIP S. NOBLE.

III. THE KNIGHT OF THE SPECTACLES TAKES THE QUILL.

This paper is writ unto her most Royal Highness, our beloved Gold Elsie, Queen of our thoughts and Empress of all hearts.

You must know, most noble Lady, that one who is your next of kin and high in the royal favor has laid upon us a most difficult and embarrassing task.

In our capacity as Director of the Court Games, we humbly suggested the subjects for the weekly bulletin which your Highness commanded to be written; but, alas, with indifferent success; for the Courtiers growled and the Ladies-in-waiting howled at the topics given them for consideration.

On soliciting our own subjects from the Privy Councilor and Knight of the Brush, Lord John Howard, he revengefully ordered me to " edify " your Majesty with wise utterances; as if such poor, rude words as mine could please the ear that should only listen to the singing of birds, the babbling of brooks, or the silvery tongue of genius!

When may your devoted subjects hope to see their gracious Sovereign again in their midst?

The court is fast drifting into dangerous informalities of conduct. The Princess Bell-Pepper partakes of the odoriferous onion at each noonday meal, so that a royal salute would be impossible; the hands of the Countess Paulina look as if you might have chosen one of your attendants from " Afric's sunny fountains, or India's coral strand; " and as for the Court Chaplain, Rev. Jack-in-the-Pulpit, he has wofully forsaken the manners of the " cloth " and

insists upon retaining his ancient title of
Knight of the Brush; the Duchess of Sweet
Marjoram alone continues circumspect in walk
and mien, for blood will tell, and she is more
Noble than the others.

In our capacity of Court Physician we have
thrice relieved your youthful page, Sir Dicky
Winship, of indigestion, caused by too generous indulgence in the flowing bowl — of milk
and cherries; we have also prescribed for his
grace the Duke of Noble, whose ducal ear was
poisoned by the insidious oak leaf.

Your private box awaits you in the Princess'
Theatre, and your Majesty's special interpreters
of the drama will celebrate your arrival as gor-
geously as it deserves.

The health of our dearly beloved Sovereign
engages the constant thought of all her loyal
and adoring subjects; they hope, ere long to
cull a wreath of laurel with their own hands
and place it on a brow which needs naught but
its golden crown of hair to affirm its queenly
dignity. And as for crown jewels, has not
our Empress of Hearts a full store? — two dazzling sapphires, her eyes; a string of pearls,
her teeth; her lips two rubies; and when she
opens them, diamonds of wisdom issue there-
from!

Come ! and let the sight of thy royal
charms gladden the eyes of thy waiting people ! Issued under the hand of

SIR GEOFFREY STRONG, Bart.,
Court Physician and Knight of the Spectacles.

IV. MARGERY'S CONTRIBUTION.

COSY NOOK, *July* 11, 188–

MY OWN DEAR ELSIE, — Your weekly chronicle is almost ready for Monday's stage, and I
am allowed to come in at the close with as
many pages of " gossip " as I choose ; which
means that I may run on to my heart's content
and tell you all the little things that happen in the chinks between the great ones, for
uncle Doc has refused to read this part of the
letter.

First for some commissions : aunt Truth asks
if your mother will kindly select goods and
engage Mrs. Perkins to make us each a couple
of Scotch gingham dresses. She has our meas-
ures and we wish them simple, full skirted
gowns, like the last ; everybody thinks them so
pretty and becoming. Bell's two must be buff
and pink, Polly's gray and green, and mine
blue and brown. We find that we have n't
clothes enough for a three months' stay ; and
the out-of-door life is so hard upon our " forest

suits " that we have asked Mrs. Perkins to send us new ones as soon as possible.

We have had a very busy and exciting week since Polly began this letter, for there have been various interruptions and an unusual number of visitors.

First, there was our mountain climb to the top of Pico Negro; Phil says he has written you about that, but I hardly believe he mentioned that he and the other boys worried us sadly by hanging on to the tails of our horses as they climbed up the steepest places. To be sure they were so awfully tired that I could n't help pitying them; but uncle Doc had tried to persuade them not to walk, so that it was their own fault after all. You cannot imagine what a dreadful feeling it gives one, to be climbing a slippery rocky path, and know that a great heavy boy is pulling your horse backwards by the tail. Polly insisted that she heard her mule's tail break loose from its moorings, and on measuring it when we got back to camp she found it three inches longer than usual.

The mule acted like original sin all day, and Polly was so completely worn out that she went to bed at five o'clock; Jack was a good deal the worse for wear too, so that they got on beautifully all day. It is queer that they irri-

tate each other so, for I am sure that there is
no lack of real friendship between them; but
Jack is a confirmed tease and he seems to keep
all his mischief bottled up for especial use with
Polly. I have tried to keep him out of trouble, as you asked me; and although it gives me
plenty to do, I am succeeding tolerably well,
except in his dealings with Polly. I lecture
him continually, but " every time he opens his
mouth he put his foot in it."

Polly was under a cloud the first of the
week. Villikins was sick, and Dr. Winship
sent her to aunt Truth for a bottle of sweet oil.
Aunt Truth was not in sight, so Polly went to
the box of stores and emptied a whole quart
bottle of salad oil into a pail, and Villikins
had to take it, *wheel or whoa* (Jack's joke!)
Auntie went to make the salad dressing at dinner-time, and discovered her loss and Polly's
mistake. It was the last bottle; and as we
can't get any more for a week, the situation
was serious, and she was very much tried. Poor
Polly had a good cry over her carelessness, and
came to the dinner-table in a very sensitive
frame of mind. Then what should Jack do
but tell Dicky to take Villikins a head of lettuce for his supper, and ask Polly why she
did n't change his name from Villikins to

Salad-in! Polly burst into tears, and left the table, while Dr. Paul gave Jack a scolding, which I really think he deserved, though it was a good joke. The next morning, the young gentleman put on a pair of old white cotton gloves and his best hat, gathered her a bouquet of wild flowers, and made her a handsome apology before the whole party; so she forgave him, and they are friends — until the next quarrel.

On the night before the play, Laura and Scott Burton arrived on horseback, and the next morning the rest of the family appeared on the scene. We had sent over to see if Laura would play Audrey on so short notice, and bring over some odds and ends for costumes. We actually had an audience of sixteen persons, and we had no idea of playing before anybody but aunt Truth and Dicky.

There were three of the Burtons, Pancho, Hop Yet, the people from the dairy farm, and a university professor from Berkeley, with eight students. They were on a walking tour, and were just camping for the night when Scott and Jack met them, and invited them over to the performance. Geoffrey and Phil were acquainted with three of them, and uncle Paul knew the professor.

Laura, Anne, and Scott went home the next morning, but came back in two days for their week's visit. The boys like Scott very much; he falls right into the camp ways, and does n't disturb the even current of our life; and Anne, who is a sweet little girl of twelve, has quite taken Dicky under her wing, much to our relief.

With Laura's advent, however, a change came over the spirit of our dreams, and, to tell the truth, we are not over and above pleased with it. By the way, she spent last summer at the hotel, and you must have seen her, did you not? Anyway, Mrs. Burton and aunt Truth were old school friends, and Bell has known Laura for two years, but they will never follow in their mothers' footsteps. Laura is so different from her mother that I should never think they were relations; and she has managed to change all our arrangements in some mysterious way which we can't understand. I get on very well with her; she positively showers favors upon me, and I more than half suspect it is because she thinks I don't amount to much. As for the others, she rubs Polly the wrong way, and I believe she is a little bit jealous of Bell.

You see, she is several months older than

the rest of us, and has spent two winters in San Francisco, where she went out a great deal to parties and theatres, so that her ideas are entirely different from ours.

She wants every single bit of attention, — one boy to help her over the brooks, one to cut walking-sticks for her, another to peel her oranges, and another to read Spanish with her, and so on. Now, you know very well that she will never get all this so long as Bell Winship is in camp, for the boys think that Bell drags up the sun when she 's ready for him in the morning, and pushes him down at night when she happens to feel sleepy.

We, who have known Bell always, cannot realize that any one can help loving her, but there is something in Laura which makes it impossible for her to see the right side of people. She told me this morning that she thought Bell had grown so vain and airy and self-conscious that it was painful to see her. I could not help being hurt; for you know what Bell is, — brimful of nonsense and sparkle and bright speeches, but just as open as the day and as warm as the sunshine. If she could have been spoiled, we should have turned her head long ago; but she has n't a bit of silly vanity, and I never met any one before who did n't see the

pretty charm of her brightness and goodness,
did you?

And yet, somehow, Laura sticks needles
into her every time she speaks. She feels
them too, but it only makes her quiet, for she
is too proud and sensitive to resent it. I can
see that she is different in her ways, as if she
felt she was being criticised. Polly is quite
the reverse. If anybody hurts her feelings
she makes creation scream, and I admire her
courage.

Aunt Truth does n't know anything about
all this, for Laura is a different girl when she
is with her or Dr. Paul; not that she is deceit-
ful, but that she is honestly anxious for their
good opinion. You remember aunt Truth's
hobby that we should never defend ourselves
by attacking any one else, and none of us would
ever complain, if we were hung, drawn, and
quartered.

Laura was miffed at having to play Audrey,
but we did n't know that she could come until
the last moment, and we were going to leave
that part out.

"I don't believe you appreciate my generosity in taking this thankless part," she said
to Bell, when we were rehearsing. "Nobody
would ever catch you playing second fiddle,

my dear. All leading parts reserved for Miss Winship, by order of the authors, I suppose."

"Indeed, Laura," Bell said, "if we had known you were coming we would have offered you the best part, but I only took Rosalind because I knew the lines, and the girls insisted."

"You've trained the girls well, — has n't she, Geoffrey," asked Laura, with a queer kind of laugh.

But I will leave the unpleasant subject. I should not have spoken of it at all except that she has made me so uncomfortable to-day that it is fresh in my mind. Bell and Polly and I have talked the matter all over, and are going to try and make her like us, whether she wants to or not. We have agreed to be just as polite and generous as we possibly can, and see if she won't "come round," for she is perfectly delighted with the camp, and wants to stay a month.

Polly says she is going to sing "Home, Sweet Home" to her every night, and drop double doses of the homœopathic cure for home-sickness into her tea, with a view of creating the disease.

Good-by, and a hundred kisses from your loving

MARGERY DAW.

V. THE CAMP POETESS ADDS HER STORE OF MENTAL
RICHES TO THE GENERAL FUND.

My Darling, — I have a thousand things to
tell you, but I cannot possibly say them in
rhyme, merely because the committee insists
upon it. I send you herewith all the poetry
which has been written in camp since last
Monday, and it has been a very prosy week.

I have given them to papa, and he says that
the best of my own, which are all bad enough,
is the following hammock-song.

I thought it out while I was swinging Margery, and here it is ! —

> To — fro,
> Dreamily, slow,
> Under the trees ;
> Swing — swing,
> Drowsily sing
> The birds and the bees ;
> Sleep — rest,
> Slumber is best,
> Wakefulness sad ;
> Rest — sleep,
> Forget how to weep,
> Dream and be glad !

Papa says it is all nonsense to say that slumber is best and wakefulness sad; and that it is
possible to tell the truth in poetry. Perhaps it
is, but why don't they do it oftener, then ?

And how was he to know that Polly and Jack
had just gone through a terrible battle of words
in which I was peacemaker, and that Dicky
had been as naughty as — Nero — all day?
These two circumstances made me look at the
world through blue glasses, and that is always
the time one longs to write poetry.

I send you also Geoff's verses, written to
mamma, and slipped into the box when we
were playing Machine Poetry : —

> I know a woman fair and calm,
> Whose shining tender eyes
> Make, when I meet their earnest gaze,
> Sweet thoughts within me rise.
>
> And if all silver were her hair,
> Or faded were her face,
> She would not look to me less fair,
> Nor lack a single grace.
>
> And if I were a little child,
> With childhood's timid trust,
> I think my heart would fly to her,
> And love — because it must !
>
> And if I were an earnest man,
> With empty heart and life,
> I think — (but I might change my mind)
> She 'd be my chosen wife !

Is n't that pretty? Oh, Elsie ! I hope I
shall grow old as beautifully as mamma does,
so that people can write poetry to me if they

feel like it! Here is Jack's, for Polly's birth-day ; he says he got the idea from a real poem which is just as silly as his : —

A pollywog from a wayside brook
Is a goodly gift for thee ;
But a milk-white steed, or a venison sheep,
Will do very well for me.

For you a quivering asphodel,
(Two ducks and a good fat hen,)
For me a withering hollyhock
(For seven and three are ten !)

Rose-red locks and a pug for thee,
(The falling dew is chill,)
A dove, a rope, and a rose for me,
(Oh, passionate, pale-blue pill !)

For you a greenery, yallery gown,
(Hath one tomb room for four ?)
Dig me a narrow gravelet here,
(Oh, red is the stain of gore ! !)

I told Jack I thought it extremely unhitched, but he says that's the chief beauty of the imi-tation.

I give you also some verses intended for Polly's birthday, which we shall celebrate, when the day arrives, by a grand dinner.

You remember how we tease her about her love for tea, which she cannot conceal, but which she is ashamed of all the same.

Well ! I have printed the poem on a card,

and on the other side Margery has drawn the picture of a cross old maid, surrounded by seven cats, all trying to get a drink out of her tea-cup.   Then Geoff is going to get a live cat from the milk ranch near here and box it up for me to give to her when she receives her presents at the dinner-table.   Won't it be fun?

OWED TO POLLY

BECAUSE OF HER BIRTHDAY.

She camps among the untrodden ways
    Forninst the "Mountain Mill;"
A maid whom there are few to praise
    And few to wish her ill.

She lives unknown, and few could know
    What Pauline is to me;
As dear a joy as are to her,
    Her frequent cups of tea.

A birthday this dear creature had,
    Full many a year ago;
She says she is but just fifteen,
    Of course she ought to know.

But still this gift I bring to her,
    Appropriate to her age,
Regardless of her stifled scorn,
    Or well conceal-ed rage!

She smiles upon these tender lines,
    As you all plainly see,
But when she meets me all alone,
    How different it will be!

Now comes Geoff's, to be given with a pretty little inkstand : —

> There was a young maiden whose thought
> Was so airy it could n't be caught;
>   So what do you think?
>   We gave her some ink,
> And captured her light-wingéd thought.

Here is Jack's last on Polly : —

> There 's a pert little poppet called Polly,
> Who frequently falls into folly!
>   She 's a terrible tongue,
>   For a "creetur" so young,
> But if she were dumb she 'd be jolly!

I helped Polly with a reply and we delivered it five minutes later : —

> I 'd rather be deaf, Master Jack,
> For if only one sense I must lack,
>   To be rid of your voice,
>   I should always rejoice,
> Nor mourn if it never came back!

And now good night and good-by until I am allowed to write you my own particular kind of letter.

The girls and boys are singing round the camp fire, and I must go out and join them in one song before we go to bed.

Yours with love, now and always,

BELL.

P. S. — Our "Happy Hexagon" has become

a sort of " Obstreperous Octagon." Laura and
Scott Burton are staying with us. Scott is a
good deal of a bookworm and uses very long
words; his favorite name for me at present is
Calliope; I thought it was a sort of steam
whistle, but Margery thinks it was some one
who was connected with poetry. We don't
dare ask the boys; will you find out?

VI.

Camp Chaparral, *July* 13, 188–.
Studio Raphael.

DEAR LITTLE SIS, — The inclosed sketches
speak for themselves, or at least I hope they do.
Keep them in your private portfolio, and when
I am famous you can produce them to show
the public at what an early age my genius
began to sprout.

At first I thought I'd make them real
" William Henry " pictures, but concluded to
give you a variety.

Can't stop to write another line; and if
you missed your regular letter this week you
must not growl, for the sketches took an awful
lot of time, and I'm just rushed to death here
anyway.

Love to mother and father.

Your loving brother, JACK.

P. S. — Polly says you need not expect to recognize that deer by his portrait, should you ever meet him, as no one could expect to get a *striking* likeness at a distance of a half mile. But, honestly, we have been closer than that to several deer.

CHAPTER V.

THE FOREST OF ARDEN. — GOOD NEWS.

> " From the East to western Ind,
>   No jewel is like Rosalind ;
>   Her worth, being mounted on the wind,
>   Through all the world bears Rosalind ;
>   All the pictures, fairest lined,
>   Are but black to Rosalind ;
>   Let no face be kept in mind,
>   But the fair of Rosalind."

THE grand performance of " As You Like It" must have a more extended notice than it has yet received, inasmuch as its double was never seen on any stage.

The reason of this somewhat ambitious selection lay in the fact that our young people had studied it in Dr. Winship's Shakespeare class the preceding winter, but they were actually dumb with astonishment when Bell proposed it for the opening performance in the new theatre.

" I tell you," she argued, " there are not many pieces which would be effective when played out of doors by dim candle-light, but this will be just as romantic and lovely as can be. You see it can be played just 'as you like it.' "

Philip and aunt Truth wanted a matinée performance, but the girls resisted this plan very strongly, feeling that the garish light of day would be bad for the makeshift costumes, and would be likely to rob them of what little courage they possessed.

" We give the decoration of the theatre entirely into your hands, boys," Polly had said, on the day before the performance. " You have some of the hardest work done already, and can just devote yourselves to the ornamental part ; but don't expect any more ideas from us, for you will certainly be disappointed."

" I should think not, indeed ! " cried Bell, energetically. " Here we have the wall decorations for the first scene, and all the costumes besides ; and the trouble is, that three or four of them will have to be made to-morrow, after Laura comes with the trappings of war. I

hope she will get here for dinner to-night;
then we can decide on our finery, and have a
rough rehearsal."

" Well, girls!" shouted Jack, from the theatre, " come and have one consultation, and
then we 'll let you off. Phil wants to change
the location altogether."

" Oh, nonsense!" cried Madge, as the three
girls ran towards the scene of action. " It 's
the only suitable place within a mile of the
camp."

" I think it will be simply perfect, when you
have done a little more cutting," said Bell.
" Just see our advantages : First, we have that
rising knoll opposite the stage, which is exactly
the thing for audience-seats; then we have
a semicircular background of trees and a flat
place for the stage, which is perfectly invalua-
ble; last of all, just gaze upon that madroño-
tree in the centre, and the oak on the left; why,
they are worth a thousand dollars for scenery."

" Especially in the first scene, — ducal interior, or whatever it is," said Phil, disconsolately.

" Jingo! that is a little embarrassing,"
groaned Jack.

" Not at all," said Polly, briskly. " There
is plenty of room to set the interior in front of
those trees. It can be all fixed beforehand,

and just whisked away for good at the end of
the first act."

"That's true," said Geoff, thoughtfully.
"But we can't have any Adam's cottage. We
talked it over last night, and decided it
'couldn't be did.'"

"Did you, indeed!" exclaimed Bell, sarcastically. "Then allow me to remark that you
three boys represent a very obtuse triangle."

"Thanks, most acid Rosalind!" murmured
Geoff, meekly. "Could you deign, as spokesman of the very acute triangle, to suggest
something?"

"Certainly. There is the rear of the brush
kitchen in plain sight, to convey the idea of a
rustic hut. To be sure, it's a good distance
to the left, but let the audience screw round in
their seats when they hear the voices, and
Adam, Oliver, and Orlando can walk out carelessly, and go through their scene right there."

"Admirable!" quoth Geoff. "We bow to
your superior judgment."

"What an inspiration that was to bring
those Chinese lanterns for the Fourth of July;
they have just saved us from utter ruin," said
Margery, who was quietly making leaf-trim-
ming.

"Yes, the effect is going to be perfectly

gorgeous ! " exclaimed Polly, clasping her hands in anticipation. " How many have we? Ten? Oh, that's splendid! and how many candles?"

" As many as we care to use," Phil answered, from the top of the ladder where he was at work. " And look at my arrangement for holding them to these trees. Are n't they immense?"

" By the way," said Bell, " don't forget the mossy banks under those trees, for stage seats; and make me some kind of a thing on the left side, to swoon on when I sniff Orlando's gory handkerchief."

" A couple of rocks," suggested Jack.

" Not exactly," replied the critical Rosalind, with great dignity. " I am black and blue already from practicing my faint, and I expect to shriek with pain when I fall to-morrow night."

" St. Jacob's oil relieves stiffened joints, smoothes the wrinkles from the brow of care, soothes lacerated feelings, and 'ushes the 'owl of hinfancy," remarked Geoffrey serenely, as he prepared to build the required mossy banks.

" My dear cousin (there are times when I am glad it is only second cousin), have you a secret contract to advertise a vulgar patent medicine? or why this eloquence?" laughed Bell.

"And, Jack," suggested Polly, "you don't seem to be doing anything; fix a stump for me to sit on while Orlando and Rosalind are making love."

"All right, countess. I'd like to see you stumped once in my life. Shall we have the canvases brought for stage carpets?"

"We say no," cried Rosalind, firmly. "We shall be a thousand times more awkward stumbling over stiff billows of carpet. Let's sweep the ground as clean and smooth as possible, and let it go for all the scenes."

"Yes, we shall then be well *grounded* in our parts," remarked Phil, hiding his head behind a bunch of candles.

"Take care, young man," laughed Polly, " or you may be ' run to earth,' instead."

"Or be requested by the audience to get up and dust," cried the irrepressible Jack, whose wit was very apt to be of a slangy character. "Now let us settle the interior, or I shall go mad."

"Bell and I have it all settled," said Geoffrey, promptly. " The background is to be made of three sheets hung over a line, and the two sides will be formed of canvas carpets; the walls will have Japanese fans, parasols, and " —

"Jupiter!" exclaimed Jack, who, as knight

of the brush, felt compelled to be artistic. "Imagine a ducal palace, in the year so many hundred and something, decorated with Japanese bric-a-brac! I blush for you."

"Now, Jack, we might as well drop the whole play as begin to think of the 'nakkeronisms,' or whatever the word is. I have got to wear an old white wrapper to the wrestling-match, but I don't complain," said Polly.

Just here Bell ran back from the kitchen, exclaiming, —

"I have secured Pancho for Charles the wrestler. Oh, he was fearfully obstinate! but when I told him he would only be on the stage two minutes, and would not have to speak a word, but just let Geoff throw him, he consented. Isn't that good? Did you decide about the decorations?"

"It will have to be just as we suggested," answered Margery. "Fans, parasols, flowers, and leaves, with the madroño-wood furniture scattered about, sheep-skins, etc."

"A few venison rugs, I presume you mean," said Geoffrey, slyly. "Say, Polly, omit the cold cream for once, will you? You don't want to outshine everybody."

"Thank you," she replied. "I will endeavor to take care of my own complexion, if you will allow me. As for yours, you look more like Othello than Orlando."

"Come, come, girls," said industrious Margery, "let us go to the tent and sew. It is nothing but nonsense here, and we are not accomplishing anything."

So they wisely left the boys to themselves for the entire day, and transformed their tent into a mammoth dressmaking establishment, with clever aunt Truth as chief designer.

The intervening hours had slipped quickly away, and now the fatal moment had arrived, and everything was ready for the play.

The would-be actresses were a trifle excited when the Professor and his eight students were brought up and introduced by Jack and Scott Burton ; and, as if that were not enough, who should drive up at the last moment but the family from the neighboring milk ranch, and beg to be allowed the pleasure of witnessing the performance. Mr. Sandford was the gentleman who had sold Dr. Winship his land, and so they were cordially invited to remain.

All the cushions and shawls belonging to the camp were arranged carefully on the knoll, for audience seats ; it was a brilliant moonlight night, and the stage assumed a very festive appearance with its four pounds of candles and twelve Chinese lanterns.

Meanwhile the actors were dressing in their respective tents. Bell's first dress was a long pink muslin wrapper of Mrs. Burton's, which had been belted in and artistically pasted over with bouquets from the cretonne trunk covers, in imitation of flowered satin; under this she wore a short blue lawn skirt of her own, catching up the pink muslin on the left side with a bouquet of wild roses, and producing what she called "a positively Neilson effect."

Her bright hair was tossed up into a fluffy knot on the top of her head; and with a flat coronet of wild roses and another great bunch at her belt, one might have gone far and not have found a prettier Rosalind.

"I declare, you are just too lovely — is n't she Laura?" asked Margery.

"Yes, she looks quite well," answered Laura, abstractedly, being much occupied in making herself absurdly beautiful as Audrey. "Of course the dress fits horridly, but perhaps it won't show in the dim light."

"Oh, is it very bad?" sighed Bell plaintively; "I can't see it in this glass. Well, the next one fits better, and I have to wear that the longest. Shall I do your hair, Laura?"

"No — thanks; Margery has such a capital knack at hair-dressing, and she does n't come on yet."

During this conversation Polly was struggling with aunt Truth's trained white wrapper. It was rather difficult to make it look like a court dress; but she looked as fresh and radiant as a rose in it, for the candle-light obliterated every freckle, and one could see nothing but a pair of dancing eyes, the pinkest of cheeks, and a head running over with curls of ruddy gold.

"Now, Bell, criticise me!" she cried, taking a position in the middle of the tent, and turning round like a wax figure. "I have torn out my hair by the roots to give it a 'done up' look, and have I succeeded? and shall I wear any flowers with this lace surplice? and what on earth shall I do with my hands? they 're so black they will cast a gloom over the stage. Perhaps I can wrap my handkerchief carelessly round one, and I 'll keep the other round your waist, considerable, tucked under your Watteau pleat.   Will I do?"

"Do?   I should think so!" and Bell eyed her with manifest approval. "Your hair is very nice, and your neck looks lovely with that lace handkerchief. As for flowers, why don't you wear a great mass of yellow and white daisies? You 'll be as gorgeous as" —

" As a sunset by Turner," said Laura with a glance at Polly's auburn locks. "Seems to me this is a mutual admiration society, is n't it?" and she sank languidly into a chair to have her hair dressed.

" Yes, it is," cried Polly, boldly; "and it 's going to 'continner.' Meg, you 're a darling in that blue print and pretty hat. I 'll fill my fern-basket with flowers, and you can take it, so as to have something in your hand to play with. You look nicer than any Phœbe I ever saw, that 's a fact. And now, hurrah! we 're all ready, and there 's the boys' bell, so let us assemble out in the kitchen. Oh dear! I believe I 'm frightened, in spite of every promise to the contrary."

When the young people saw each other for the first time in their stage costumes, there was a good deal of merriment and some honest admiration. Geoff looked very odd without his eyeglasses and with the yellow wig that was the one property belonging to this star dramatic organization.

The girls had not succeeded in producing a great effect with the masculine costumes, because of insufficient material. But the boys

had determined not to wear their ordinary
clothes, no matter what happened; so Jack had
donned one of Hop Yet's blue blouses for his
Sylvius dress, and had ready a plaid shawl to
throw gracefully over one shoulder whenever
he changed to the Banished Duke.

His Sylvius attire was open to criticism, but
no one could fail to admire his appearance as
the Duke, on account of a magnificent ducal
head-gear, from which soared a bunch of tall
peacock feathers.

"Oh, Jack, what a head-dress for a Duke!"
laughed Margery; "no wonder they banished
you. Did you offend the court hatter?"

Phil said that at all events nobody could
mistake him for anything but a fool, in his
"Touchstone" costume, and so he was jest-er
going to be contented.

Scott Burton was arranging Pancho's toilette
for the wrestling-match, and meanwhile trying
to raise his drooping spirits; and Rosalind was
vainly endeavoring to make Adam's beard of
gray moss stay on.

While these antics were going on behind the
scenes, the audience was seated on the knoll,
making merry over the written programmes,
which had been a surprise of Geoff's, and read
as follows: —

THE PRINCESS' THEATRE.
July 10th, 188–.

———

APPEARANCE OF THE GREATEST DRAMATIC COMPANY ON EARTH (FACT).

THE COOLEST THEATRE IN THE WORLD.

———

A Royal Galaxy and *Boyaxy* of Artists in the play of

AS YOU LIKE IT,

By William Shakespeare, or Lord Bacon.

———

CAST.

" Alas ! unmindful of their doom, the little victims play ;
No sense have they of ills to come, or cares beyond to-day."

ROSALIND	The Lady Bell-Pepper.
	(Her greatest creation.)
CELIA	The Countess Paulina.
PHŒBE . . .	The Duchess of Sweet Marjoram.
AUDREY . .	A talented Incognita of the Court.
ORLANDO . .	Hennery Irving Salvini Strong.
	(Late from the Blank Theatre, Oil City.)
ADAM	Dr. Paul Winship.
	(By kind permission of his manager, Mrs. T. W.)

BANISHED DUKE }
SYLVIUS   } Lord John Howard }   Lightning
TOUCHSTONE }   Duke of Noble } Change Artists.
JACQUES   }

(N. B. The Duke of Noble has played the " fool " five million times.)

OLIVER . . . . . . Mr. Scott Burton.
(Specially engaged.)

CHARLES THE WRESTLER . Pancho Muldoon Sullivan.
(His first appearance.)

The Comb Orchestra will play the Music of the Future.
The Usher will pass pop-corn between the Acts.
Beds may be ordered at 10.30.

The scene between Adam and Orlando went off with good effect; and when Celia and Rosalind came through the trees in an affectionate attitude, and Celia's blithe voice broke the stillness with, "I pray thee Rosalind, sweet my coz, be merry," there was a hearty burst of applause which almost frightened them into silence.

At the end of the first act everybody was delighted; the stage-manager, carpenter, scene-shifter, costumer, and all the stars were called successively before the curtain.

Hop Yet declared it was "all the same good as China theatre;" and every one agreed to that criticism without a dissenting voice.

To be sure, there was an utter absence of stage-management, and all the "traditions" were remarkable for their absence; but I fancy that the spirits of Siddons and Kemble, Macready and Garrick, looked down with kind approval upon these earnest young actors as they recited the matchless old words, moving to and fro in the quaint setting of trees and moonlight, with an orchestra of cooing doves and murmuring zephyrs.

The forest scenes were intended to be the

features of the evening, and in these the young
people fairly surpassed themselves. Any one
who had seen Neilson in her doublet and hose
of silver-gray, Modjeska in her shades of blue,
and Ada Cavendish in her lovely suit of green,
might have thought Bell's patched-up dress a
sorry mixture; yet these three brilliant stars in
the theatrical firmament might have envied this
little Rosalind the dewy youth and freshness
that so triumphed over all deficiencies of costume.

Margery's camping-dress of gray, shortened
to the knee, served for its basis. Round the
skirt and belt and sleeves were broad bands of
laurel-leaf trimming. She wore a pair of Margery's long gray stockings and Laura's dainty
bronze Newport ties. A soft gray chudda
shawl of aunt Truth's was folded into a mantle
to swing from the shoulder, its fringes being
caught up out of sight, and a laurel-leaf trimming added. On her bright wavy hair was
perched a cunning flat cap of leaves, and, as
she entered with Polly, leaning on her manzanita staff, and sighing, "Oh Jupiter, how weary
are my spirits!" one could not wish a lovelier
stage picture.

And so the play went on, with varying fortunes. Margery was frightened to death, and

persisted in taking Touchstone's speeches right out of his mouth, much to his discomfiture. Adam's beard refused to stay on; so did the moustache of the Banished Duke, and the clothes of Sylvius. But nothing could dampen the dramatic fire of the players, nor destroy the enthusiasm of the sympathetic audience.

Dicky sat in the dress-circle, wrapped in blankets, and laughed himself nearly into convulsions over Touchstone's jokes, and the stage business of the Banished Duke; for it is unnecessary to state that Jack was not strictly Shakespearean in his treatment of the part.

As for Polly, she enjoyed being Celia with all her might, and declared her intention of going immediately on the "regular" stage; but Jack somewhat destroyed her hopes by affirming that her nose and hair would n't be just the thing on the metropolitan boards, although they might pass muster in a backwoods theatre.

"Hello! What's this?" exclaimed Philip, one morning. "A visitor? Yes — no! Why, it's Señor Don Manuel Felipe Hilario Noriega coming up the cañon! He's got a loaded team, too! I wonder if uncle Doc is expecting anything."

The swarthy gentleman with the long name emerged from one cloud of dust and disappeared in another, until he neared the gate where Philip and Polly were standing.

Philip opened the gate, and received a bow of thanks which would have made Manuel's reputation at a Spanish court.

"Going up to camp?"

"Si, señor."

"Those things for us?"

"Si, señor."

"What are they?"

"Si, señor."

"Exactly! Well, are there any letters?"

"Si, señor." Whereupon he drew one from his gorgeously-decorated leather belt.

Philip reached for it, and Polly leaned over his shoulder, devoured with curiosity.

"It's for aunt Truth," she said; "and — yes, I am sure it is Mrs. Howard's writing; and if it is" —

Hereupon, as Manuel spoke no English, and neither Philip nor Polly could make inquiries in Spanish, Polly darted to the cart in her usual meteoric style, put one foot on the hub of a wheel and climbed to the top like a squirrel, snatched off a corner of the canvas cover, and cried triumphantly, "I knew it!

Elsie is coming! Here's a tent, and some mattresses and pillows. Hurry! Help me down, quick! Oh, slow coach! Keep out of the way and I'll jump! Give me the letter. I can run faster than you can." And before the vestige of an idea had penetrated Philip's head, nothing could be seen of Polly but a pair of twinkling heels and the gleam of a curly head that caught every ray of the sun and turned it into ruddier gold.

It was a dusty, rocky path, and up-hill at that; but Polly, who was nothing if not ardent, never slackened her pace, but dashed along until she came in sight of the camp, where she expended her last breath in one shrill shriek for aunt Truth.

It was responded to promptly. Indeed, it was the sort of shriek that always commands instantaneous attention; and aunt Truth came out of her tent prepared to receive tragic news. Bell followed; and the entire family would have done the same, had they been in camp.

Polly thrust the letter into Mrs. Winship's hand, and sank down exhausted, exclaiming, breathlessly, "There's a mattress — and a tent — coming up the cañon. — It's Elsie's, I know. — Philip is down at the gate — with the cart, — but I came ahead. — Phew! but it's warm!"

"What!" cried Bell, joyfully. "Elsie at the gate! It can't be true!" And she darted like an arrow through the trees.

"Come back! come back!" screamed Polly. "Elsie is not at the gate. Don S. D. M. F. H. N. is there with a team loaded down with things. Isn't it from Mrs. Howard, aunt Truth?"

"Yes, it is. Written this morning from Tacitas Rancho. Why, how is this? Let me see!"

TACITAS RANCHO, Monday Morning.

DEAR TRUTH, — You will be surprised to receive a letter from me, written from Tacitas. But here we are, Elsie and I; and, what is better, we are on our way to you.

("I knew it!" exclaimed the girls.)

Elsie has been growing steadily better for three weeks. The fever seems to have disappeared entirely, and the troublesome cough is so much lessened that she sleeps all night without waking. The doctor says that the camp-life will be the very best thing for her now, and will probably complete her recovery.

("Oh, joy, joy!" cried the girls.)

I need not say how gladly we followed this special prescription of our kind doctor's, nor add that we started at once —

("Oh, aunt Truth, there is nobody within a mile of the camp; can't I, *please* can't I turn one little hand-spring, just one little ladylike one?" pleaded Polly, dancing on one foot, and chewing her sun-bonnet string.

"No, dear, you can't! Keep quiet and let me read.")

Elsie would not let me tell you our plans any sooner, lest the old story of a sudden ill turn would keep us at home; and I think very likely that she longed to give the dear boys and girls a surprise.

We arrived at the Burtons' yesterday. Elsie bore the journey exceedingly well, but I would not take any risks, and so we shall not drive over until day after to-morrow morning.

("You need n't have hurried quite so fast, Polly dear.")

I venture to send the tent and its belongings ahead to-day, so that Jack may get everything to rights before we arrive.

The mattress is just the size the girls ordered; and of course I 've told Elsie nothing about the proposed furnishing of her tent.

I am bringing my little China boy with me, for I happen to think that, with the Burtons, we shall be fourteen at table. Gin is not quite a success as a cook, but he can at least wash dishes, wait at table, and help Hop Yet in various ways; while I shall be only too glad to share all your housekeeping cares, if you have not escaped them even in the wilderness.

I shall be so glad to see you again; and oh, Truth, I am so happy, so happy, that, please God, I can keep my child after all! The weary burden of dread is lifted off my heart, and I feel young again. Just think of it! My Elsie will be well and strong once more! It seems too good to be true.

Always your attached friend,
JANET HOWARD.

Mrs. Winship's voice quivered as she read the last few words, and Polly and Bell threw themselves into each other's arms and cried for sheer gladness.

"Come, come, dears! I suppose you will make grand preparations, and there is no time to lose. One of you must find somebody to help Philip unload the team. Papa and the boys have gone fishing, and Laura and Margery went with them, I think." And Mrs. Winship bustled about, literally on hospitable thoughts in-tent.

Polly tied on her sun-bonnet with determination, turned up her sleeves as if washing were

the thing to be done, and placed her arms
akimbo.

"First and foremost," said she, her eyes
sparkling with excitement, "first and foremost,
I am going to blow the horn."

"Certainly not," said aunt Truth. "Are
you crazy, Polly? It is scarcely ten o'clock,
and everybody would think it was dinner-time,
and come home at once."

"No, they 'd think something had happened
to Dicky," said Bell, "and that would bring
them in still sooner."

"Of course! I forgot. But can't I blow it
earlier than usual? Can't I blow it at half-
past eleven instead of twelve? We can't do a
thing without the boys, and they may not come
home until midnight unless we do something
desperate. Oh, delight! There's Don S. D.
M. F. H. N., and Phil has found Pancho to
help unload."

"Is n't it lucky that we decided on the place
for Elsie's tent, and saved it in case she should
ever come?" said Bell. "Now Philip and Pancho can set it up whenever they choose. And
is n't it fortunate that we three stayed at home
to-day, and refused to fish? now we can plan
everything, and then all work together when
they come back."

Meanwhile, Polly was tugging at an immense bundle, literally tooth and nail, as she alternated trembling clutches of the fingers with frantic bites at the offending knot.

Like many of her performances, the physical strength expended was out of all proportion to the result produced, and one stroke of Philip's knife accomplished more than all her ill-directed effort. At length the bundle of awning cloth stood revealed. "Oh, isn't it beautiful?" she cried, "it will be the very prettiest tent in camp; — can't I blow the horn?"

"Look, mamma," exclaimed Bell, "it is green and gray, in those pretty broken stripes, and the edge is cut in lovely scollops and bound with green braid. Won't it look pretty among the trees?"

Aunt Truth came out to join the admiring group.

"O-o-o-h!" screamed Polly. "There comes a piece of the floor. They've sent it all made, in three pieces. What fun! We'll have it all up and ready to sleep in before we blow the horn!"

"And here's a roll of straw matting," said Phil, depositing a huge bundle on the ground near the girls. "I'll cut the rope to save your teeth!"

"Green and white plaid!" exclaimed Bell. "Well! Mrs. Howard did have her wits about her!"

"Oh, do let me blow the horn!" teased the irrepressible Polly.

"Here are a looking-glass and a towel-rack and a Shaker rocking-chair," called Philip; "guess they're going to stay the rest of the summer."

"Yes, of course they wouldn't want a looking-glass if they were only going to stay a month or two," laughed Bell.

"Dear aunt Truth, if you won't let me turn a single decorous little hand-spring, or blow the horn, or do anything nice, will you let us use all that new white mosquito netting? Bell says that it has been in the storehouse for two years, and it would be just the thing for decorating Elsie's tent."

"Why, of course you may have it, Polly, and anything else that you can find. There! I hear Dicky's voice in the distance; perhaps the girls are coming."

Bell and Polly darted through the swarm of tents, and looked up the narrow path that led to the brook.

Sure enough, Margery and Laura were strolling towards home with little Anne and

Dick dangling behind, after the manner of children. Margery carried a small string of trout, and Dick the inevitable tin pail in which he always kept an unfortunate frog or two. The girls had discovered that he was in the habit of crowding the cover tightly over the pail and keeping his victims shut up for twenty-four hours, after which, he said, they were nice and tame, — so very tame, as it transpired, that they generally gave up the ghost in a few hours after their release. Margery had with difficulty persuaded him of his cruelty, and the cover had been pierced with a certain number of air-holes.

" Guess the loveliest thing that could possibly happen ! " called Bell at the top of her voice.

" Elsie has come," answered Margery in a second, nobody knew why; " let me hug her this minute ! "

" With those fish ? " laughed Polly. " No ! you 'll have to wait until day after to-morrow, and then your guess will be right. Is n't it almost too good to be true ? "

" And she is almost well," added Bell, joyfully, slipping her arm through Margery's and squeezing it in sheer delight. " Mrs. Howard says she is really and truly better. Oh, if Elsie

Howard in bed is the loveliest, dearest thing in the world, what will it be like to have her out of it and with us in all our good times!"

"Has she always been ill since you knew her?" asked Laura.

"Yes; a terrible cold left her with weakness of the lungs, and the doctors feared consumption, but thought that she might possibly outgrow it entirely if she lived in a milder climate; so Mrs. Howard left home and everybody she cared for, and brought Elsie to Santa Barbara. Papa has taken an interest in her from the first, and as far as we girls are concerned it was love at first sight. You never knew anybody like Elsie!"

"Is she pretty?"

"Pretty!" cried Polly, "she is like an angel in a picture book!"

"Interesting?"

"Interesting!" said Bell, in a tone that showed the word to be too feeble for the subject, — "Elsie is more interesting than all the other girls in the world put together!"

"Popular?"

"Popular!" exclaimed Margery, taking her turn in the oral examination, "I don't know whether anybody can be popular who is always in bed; but if it's popular to be adored by every man, woman, child, and animal that comes anywhere near her, why then Elsie is popular."

" And is she a favorite with boys as well as girls ? "

" Favorite ! " said Bell. " Why, they think that she is simply perfect ! Of course she has scarcely been able to sit up a week at a time for a year, and naturally she has not seen many people ; but if you want a boy's opinion, just ask Philip or Geoffrey. I assure you, Laura, after you have known Elsie a while and have seen the impression she makes upon everybody, you will want to go to bed and see if you can do likewise."

" It is n't just the going to bed," remarked Margery, sagely.

" And it is n't the prettiness either," added Polly ; " though if you saw Elsie asleep, a flower in one hand, the other under her cheek, her hair straying over the pillow (O for hair that would stray anywhere !), you would expect every moment to see a halo above her head."

"I don't believe it is because she is good that everybody admires her so," said Laura, " I don't think goodness in itself is always so very interesting ; if Elsie had freckles and a snub nose " (" Don't mind me ! " murmured Polly) "you would find that people would say less about her wonderful character."

"There are things that puzzle me," said Polly, thoughtfully. "It seems to me that if I could contrive to be ever so good, nobody ever would look for a halo round my head. Now, is it my turned-up nose and red hair that make me what I am, or did what I am make my nose and hair what they are, — which?"

"We 'll have to ask aunt Truth," said Margery; "that is too difficult a thing for us to answer."

"Was n't it nice I catched that big bull-frog, Margie?" cried Dick, his eyes shining with anticipation. "Now I 'll have as many as seven or 'leven frogs and lots of horned toads when Elsie comes, and she can help me play with 'em.'"

When the girls reached the tents again, the last article had been taken from the team and Manuel had driven away. The sound of Phil's hammer could be heard from the carpenter-shop, and Pancho was already laying the tent floor in a small, open, sunny place, where the low boughs of a single sycamore hung so as to protect one of its corners, leaving the rest to the full warmth of the sunshine that was to make Elsie entirely well again.

" I am tired to death," sighed Laura, throwing herself down in a bamboo lounging-chair. " Such a tramp as we had ! and after all, the boys insisted on going where Dr. Winship would n't allow us to follow, so that we had to stay behind and fish with the children ; I wish I had stayed at home and read ' The Colonel's Daughter.' "

" O Laura ! " remonstrated Margery, " think of that lovely pool with the forests of maiden-hair growing all about it ! "

" And poison oak," grumbled Laura. " I know I walked into some of it and shall look like a perfect fright for a week. I shall never make a country girl — it 's no use for me to try."

" It 's no use for you to try walking four miles in high-heeled shoes, my dear," said Polly, bluntly.

" They are not high," retorted Laura, " and if they are, I don't care to look like a — a — cow-boy, even in the backwoods."

" I 'm an awful example," sighed Polly, seating herself on a stump in front of the tent, and elevating a very dusty little common-sense boot. " Sir Walter Raleigh would never have allowed me to walk on his velvet cloak with that boot, would he girls ? Oh, was n't that romantic, though? and don't I wish that I had been Queen Elizabeth!"

"You 've got the *hair*," said Laura.

"Thank you! I had forgotten Elizabeth's hair was red; so it was. This is my court train," snatching a tablecloth that hung on a bush near by, and pinning it to her waist in the twinkling of an eye, — "this my farthingale," dangling her sunbonnet from her belt, — "this my sceptre," seizing a Japanese umbrella, — "this my crown," inverting a bright tin plate upon her curly head. "She is just alighting from her chariot, *thus;* the courtiers turn pale *thus;* (why don't you do it?) what shall be done? The Royal Feet must not be wet. 'Go round the puddle? Prit, me Lud, Ods body! Forsooth! Certainly not! Remove the puddle!' she says haughtily to her subjects. They are just about to do so, when out from behind a neighboring chaparral bush stalks a beautiful young prince with coal-black hair and rose-red cheeks. He wears a rich velvet cloak, glittering with embroidery. He sees not her crown, her hair outshines it; he sees not her sceptre, her tiny hand conceals it; he sees naught save the loathly mud. He strips off his cloak and floats it on the puddle. With a haughty but gracious bend of her head the Queen accepts the courtesy; crosses the puddle, *thus*, waves her sceptre, *thus*, and saying ' You shall hear from me by return mail, me Lud,' she vanishes within the castle. The next morning she makes Sir Walter British Minister to Florida. He departs at once with a cargo of tobacco, which he exchanges for sweet potatoes, and everybody is happy ever after."

The girls were convulsed with mirth at this historical romance, and as Mrs. Winship wiped the tears of merriment from her eyes, Polly seized the golden opportunity and dropped on her knees beside her.

"Please, aunt Truth, we can't get the white mosquito-netting because Dr. Winship has the key of the store-house in his pocket, and so — may — I — blow the horn?"

Mrs. Winship gave her consent in despair, and Polly went to the oak-tree where the horn hung and blew all the strength of her lungs into blast after blast for five minutes.

"That's all I needed," she said, on returning; " that was an escape-valve, and I shall be lady-like and well behaved the rest of the day."

CHAPTER VI.

QUEEN ELSIE VISITS THE COURT.

" An hour and friend with friend will meet,
  Lip cling to lip and hand clasp hand."

"NOW, Laura," asked Bell, when quiet was
restored, "advise us about Elsie's tent.
We want it to be perfectly lovely; and you
have such good taste!"

"Let me think," said Laura. "Oh, if she
were only a brunette instead of a blonde, we
could festoon the tent with that yellow tarlatan I brought for the play!"

"What difference does it make whether she
is dark or light?" asked Bell, obtusely.

"Why, a room ought to be as becoming as a

dress, — so Mrs. Pinkerton says. You know I saw a great deal of her at the hotel; and oh, girls! her bedroom was the most exquisite thing you ever saw! She had a French toilet-table, covered with pale blue silk and white marquise lace, — perfectly lovely, — with yards and yards of robin's-egg blue watered ribbon in bows; and on it she kept all her toilet articles, everything in hammered silver from Tiffany's, with monograms on the back, — three or four sizes of brushes, and combs, and mirrors, and a full manicure set. It used to take her two hours to dress; but it was worth it. Oh, such gorgeous tea-gowns as she had! One of old rose and lettuce was a perfect dream! She always had her breakfast in bed, you know. I think it 's delightful to have your breakfast before you get up, and dress as slowly as you like. I wish mamma would let me do it."

"What does she do after she gets dressed, in her rows of old lettuce — I mean her old rows of lettuce?" asked Polly.

"Do? Why really, Polly, you are too stupid. What do you suppose she did? What everybody else does, of course."

"Oh!" said Polly, apologetically.

"How old is Mrs. Pinkerton?" asked Margery.

"Between nineteen and twenty. There is not three years' difference in our ages, though she has been married nearly two years. It seems so funny."

"Only nineteen!" cried Bell. "Why, I always thought that she was old as the hills, — twenty-five or thirty at the very least. She always seemed tired of things."

"Well," said Laura, in a whisper intended to be too low to reach Mrs. Winship's tent, "I don't know whether I ought to repeat what was told me in confidence, but the fact is — well — she does n't like Mr. Pinkerton very well!"

The other girls, who had not enjoyed the advantages of city life and travel, looked as dazed as any scandal-monger could have desired.

"Don't like him!" gasped Polly, nearly falling off the stump. "Why, she 's married to him!"

"Where on earth were you brought up?" snapped Laura. "What difference does that make? She can't help it if she does n't happen to like her husband, can she? You can't make yourself like anybody, can you?"

"Well, did she ever like him?" asked Margery; "for she 's only been married a year or two, and it seems to me it might have lasted that long if there was anything to begin on."

" But," whispered Laura, mysteriously, " you see Mr. Pinkerton was very rich and the Dentons very poor. Mr. Denton had just died, leaving them nothing at all to live on, and poor Jessie would have had to teach school, or some dreadful thing like that. The thought of it almost killed her, she is so sensitive and so refined. She never told me so in so many words, but I am sure she married Mr. Pinkerton to save her mother from poverty; and I pity her from the bottom of my heart."

" I suppose it was noble," said Bell, in a puzzled tone, " if she could n't think of any other way, but " —

" Well, did she try very hard to think of other ways?" asked Polly. " She never looked especially noble to me. I thought she seemed like a die-away, frizzlygig kind of a girl."

" I wish, Miss Oliver, that you would be kind enough to remember that Mrs. Pinkerton is one of my most intimate friends," said Laura, sharply. " And I do wish, also, that you would n't talk loud enough to be heard all through the cañon."

The color came into Polly's cheeks, but before she could answer, Mrs. Winship walked in, stocking-basket in hand, and seated herself in the little wicker rocking-chair. Polly's clarion tones had given her a clue to the subject, and she thought the discussion needed guidance.

"You were talking about Mrs. Pinkerton, girls," she said, serenely. "You say you are fond of her, Laura dear, and it seems very ungracious for me to criticise your friend; that is a thing which most of us fail to bear patiently. But I cannot let you hold her up as an ideal to be worshiped, or ask the girls to admire as a piece of self-denial what I fear was nothing but indolence and self-gratification. You are too young to talk of these things very much; but you are not too young to make up your mind that when you agree to live all your life long with a person, you must have some other feeling than a determination not to teach school. Jessie Denton's mother, my dear Laura, would never have asked the sacrifice of her daughter's whole life; and Jessie herself would never have made it had she been less vain, proud, and luxurious in her tastes, and a little braver, more self-forgetting and industrious. These are hard words, dear, and I am sorry to use them. She has gained the riches she wanted, — the carriages and servants, and tea-gowns, and hammered silver from Tiffany's, but she looks tired and disappointed, as Bell says; and I've no doubt she is, poor girl."

"I don't think you do her justice, Mrs. Winship; I don't, indeed," said Laura.

"If you are really attached to her, Laura, don't make the mistake of admiring her faults of character, but try to find her better qualities, and help her to develop them. It is a fatal thing when girls of your age set up these false standards, and order their lives by them. There are worse things than school-teaching, yes, or even floor-scrubbing or window-washing. Lovely tea-gowns and silver-backed brushes are all very pretty and nice to have, if they are not gained at the sacrifice of something better. I should have said to my daughter, had I been Mrs. Denton, 'We will work for each other, my darling, and try to do whatever God gives us to do; but, no matter how hard life is, your heart is the most precious thing in the world, and you must never sell that, if we part with everything else.' Oh, my girls, my girls, if I could only make you believe that 'poor and content is rich, and rich enough.' I cannot bear to think of your growing year by year into the conviction that these pretty glittering things of wealth are the true gold of life which everybody seeks. Forgive me, Laura, if I have hurt your feelings."

"I know you would never hurt anybody's

feelings, if you could help it, Mrs. Winship," Laura answered, with a hint of coldness in her voice, " though I can't help thinking that you are a little hard 'on poor Jessie ; but, even then, one can surely like a person without wishing to do the very same things she does."

" Yes, that is true," said Mrs. Winship, gravely. " But one cannot constantly justify a wrong action in another without having one's own standard unconsciously lowered. What we continually excuse in other people we should be inclined by and by to excuse in ourselves. Let us choose our friends as wisely as possible, and love them dearly, helping them to grow worthier of our love at the same time we are trying to grow worthier of theirs ; because ' we live by admiration, hope, and love,' you know, but not by admiring and loving the wrong things.

" But there is the horn, and I hear the boys. Let us come to luncheon, and tell our good news of Elsie."

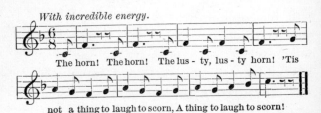

With incredible energy.

The horn! The horn! The lus - ty, lus - ty horn! 'Tis not a thing to laugh to scorn, A thing to laugh to scorn!

Long before the boys appeared in sight, their voices rang through the cañon in a chorus that woke the echoes, and presently they came into view, bearing two quarters and a saddle of freshly killed mutton, hanging from a leafy branch swung between Jack's sturdy shoulder and Geoff's.

" A splendid ' still hunt ' this morning, aunt Truth ! " exclaimed Jack. " Game plenty and not too shy, dogs in prime condition, hunters ditto. Behold the result ! "

The girls could scarcely tell whether or no Laura was offended at aunt Truth's unexpected little lecture. She did not appear quite as unrestrained as usual, but as everybody was engaged in the preparations for Elsie's welcome there was a general atmosphere of hilarity and confusion, so that no awkwardness was possible.

The tool-shop resounded with blows of hammer and steel. Dicky was under everybody's feet, and his " seven or ten frogs," together with his unrivaled collection of horned toads, were continually escaping from their tin pails and boxes in the various tents, and everybody was obliged to join in the search to recover and reincarcerate them, in order to keep the peace.

Hop Yet was making a gold and silver cake, with "Elsie" in pink letters on chocolate frosting. Philip had pitched the new tent so that in one corner there was a slender manzanita-tree which had been cropped for some purpose or other. He had nailed a cross-piece on this, so that it resembled the letter T, and was now laboriously boring holes and fitting in pegs, that Elsie might have a sort of closet behind her bed.

As for the rustic furniture, the girls and boys declared it to be too beautiful for words. They stood in circles about it and admired it without reserve, each claiming that his own special piece of work was the gem of the collection. The sunlight shining through the gray and green tints of the tent was voted perfection, Philip's closet a miracle of ingenuity, the green and white straw matting an inspiration.

The looking-glass had been mounted on a packing-box, and converted by Laura into a dressing-table that rivaled Mrs. Pinkerton's ; for green tarlatan and white mosquito netting had been so skillfully combined that the traditional mermaid might have been glad to make her toilet there "with a comb and a glass in her hand." The rest of the green and white gauzy stuff had been looped from the corners of the tent to the centre of the roof-piece, and delicate tendrils of wild clematis climbed here and there as if it were growing, its roots plunged in cunningly hidden bottles of water. Bell had gone about with pieces of awning cloth and green braid, and stitched an elaborate system of pockets on the inside of the tent wherever they would not be too prominent. There were tiny pockets for needle-work, thimbles, and scissors, medium-sized pockets for soap and combs and brushes, bigger pockets for shoes and slippers and stockings, and mammoth pockets for anything else that Elsie might ordain to put in a pocket.

By four o'clock in the afternoon Margery had used her clever fingers to such purpose that a white silesia flag, worked with the camp name, floated from the tip top of the front entrance to the tent. The ceremony of raising the flag was attended with much enthusiasm, and its accomplishment greeted by a deafening cheer from the entire party.

" Unless one wants Paradise," sighed Margery, " who would n't be contented with dear Camp Chaparral?"

" Who would live in a house, any way?" exclaimed Philip. " Sniff this air, and look up at that sky!"

"And this is what they call ' roughing it,' in Santa Barbara," quoth Dr. Winship. "Why, you youngsters have made that tent fit for the occupancy of a society belle."

"Now let's organize for reception!" cried Geoffrey. "Assemble, good people! Come over here, aunt Truth! I will take the chair myself, since I don't happen to see anybody who would fill it with more dignity."

"I am going to mount my broncho and go out on the road to meet my beloved family," said Jack, sauntering up to the impromptu council chamber.

"How can you tell when they will arrive?" asked Mrs. Winship.

"I can make a pretty good guess. They'll probably start from Tacitas as early as eight or nine o'clock, if Elsie is well. Let's see: it's about twenty-five miles, isn't it, uncle Doc? Say twenty-three to the place where they turn off the main road. Well, I'll take a bit of lunch, ride out ten or twelve miles, hitch my horse in the shade, and wait."

"Very well," said Geoffrey. "It is not usual for committees to appoint themselves, but as you are a near relative of our distinguished guests we will grant you special consideration and order you to the front. Ladies and gentlemen, passing over the slight informality of the nomination, all in favor of appointing Mr. John Howard Envoy Extraordinary please manifest it by the usual sign."

Six persons yelled " Ay," four raised the right hand, and one stood up.

" There seems to be a slight difference of opinion as to the usual sign. All right. Contrary minded ! "

" No ! " shouted Polly, at the top of her lungs.

" It is a unanimous vote," said Geoffrey, crushingly, bringing down his fist as an imaginary gavel with incredible force and dignity. " Dr. and Mrs. Winship, will you oblige the Chair by acting as a special Reception Committee ? "

" Certainly," responded the doctor, smilingly. " Will the Chair kindly outline the general policy of the committee ? "

" Hm—m—m ! Yes, certainly, — of course. The Chair suggests that the Reception Committee — well, that they stay at home and — receive the guests, — yes, that will do very nicely. All-in-favor-and-so-forth-it-is-a-vote-and-so-ordered. Secretary will please spread a copy on the minutes." Gavel.

" I rise to a point of order," said Jack, sagely.

"There is no secretary and there are no minutes."

"Mere form," said the Chair, — "sit down; there will be minutes in a minute, — got to do some more things first; that will do, *sit down.* Will the Misses Burton and Messrs. Burton and Noble kindly act as Committee on Decoration?"

"Where's the Committee on Music, and Refreshments, and Olympian Games, and all that sort of thing?" interrupted Polly, who had not the slightest conception of parliamentary etiquette; "and why don't you hurry up and put me on something?"

"If Miss Oliver refuses to bridle her tongue, and persists in interrupting the business of the meeting, the Chair will be obliged to remove her," said Geoffrey, with chilling emphasis.

Polly rose again, undaunted. "I would respectfully ask the Chair, who put him in the chair, any way?"

"Question!" roared Philip.

"Second the motion!" shrieked Bell, that being the only parliamentary expression she knew.

"Order!" cried Geoffrey in stentorian accents. "I will adjourn the meeting and clear the court-room unless there is order."

"Do!" remarked Polly, encouragingly. "I will rise again, like Phœbus, from my ashes, to say that" —

Here Jack sprang to his feet. "I would suggest to the Chair that the last speaker amend her motion by substituting the word 'Phœnix' for 'Phœbus.'"

"Accept the amendment," said Polly serenely, amidst the general hilarity.

"Question!" called Bell, with another mighty projection of memory into a missionary meeting that she had once attended.

"I am not aware that there is any motion before the house," said Geoffrey, cuttingly.

"Second the motion!" "Second the amendment!" shouted the girls.

"Ladies, there *is* no motion. Will you oblige the Chair by remaining quiet until speech is requested?"

"Move that the meeting be adjourned and another one called, with a new Chair!" remarked Margery, who felt that the honor of her sex was at stake.

"Move that this motion be so ordered and spread upon the minutes, and a copy of it be presented to the Chairman," suggested Philip.

"Move that the copy be appropriately bound in *calf*," said Jack, dodging an imaginary blow.

"Move that the other committees be elected by ballot," concluded Scott Burton.

"This is simply disgraceful!" exclaimed the Chair. "Order! order! I appoint Miss Oliver Committee on Entertainment, with a view of keeping her still."

This was received with particular as well as general satisfaction.

"Miss Winship, we appoint you Committee on Music."

"All right. Do you wish it to be original?"

"Certainly not; we wish it to be good."

"But we only know one chorus, and that's 'My Witching Dinah Snow.'"

"Never mind; either write new words to that tune or sing tra-la-la to it. Mr. Richard Winship, the Chair appoints you Committee on Menagerie, and suggests that as we have proclaimed a legal holiday, you give your animals the freedom of the city."

"Don't know what freedom of er city means," said Dicky, who feared that he was being made the butt of ridicule.

"Why, we want you to allow the captives to parade in the evening, with torch-lights and mottoes."

"All right!" cried Dicky, kindling in an

instant; " 'n' Luby, 'n' the doat, 'n' my horn'
toads, all e'cept the one that just gotted away
in Laura's bed; but may be she 'll find him to-
night, so they 'll be all there."

This was too much for the various committees, and Laura's wild shriek was the signal for
a hasty adjournment. A common danger restored peace to the assembly, and they sought
the runaway in perfect harmony.

" Well," said Jack, when quiet was restored,
" I am going a little distance up the Pico
Negro trail: there are some magnificent Spanish
bayonets growing there, and if you 'll let me
have Pancho, uncle Doc, we can bring down
four of them and lash them to each of the
corners of Elsie's tent, — they 'll keep fresh
several days in water, you know."

" Take him, certainly," said Dr. Winship.

" Do let me go with you!" pleaded Laura,
with enthusiasm. " I should like the walk so
much."

" It 's pretty rough, Laura," objected Margery. " If you could n't endure our walk this
morning, you would never get home alive from
Pico Negro."

" Oh, that was in the heat of the day," she
answered. " I feel equal to any amount of walking now, if Jack does n't mind taking me."

"Delighted, of course, Miss Laura. You'll be willing to carry home one of the trees, I suppose, in return for the pleasure of my society?"

"Snub him severely, Laura," cried Bell; "we never allow him to say such things unreproved."

"I think he is snubbed too much already," replied Laura, with a charming smile, "and I shall see how a course of encouragement will affect his behavior."

> "That will be what I long have sought,
> And mourned because I found it not,"

sang Jack nonchalantly.

"Oh, Laura," remonstrated Bell, "think twice before you encourage him in his dreadful ways. We have studied him very carefully, and we know that the only way to live with him is to keep him in a sort of 'pint pot' where we can hold the lid open just a little, and clap it down suddenly whenever he tries to spring out."

"Do not mind that young person, Miss Laura, but form your own impressions of my charming character. Excuse me, please, while I put on a celluloid collar, and make some few changes in my toilet necessary to a proper appearance in your distinguished company."

"I prefer you as you are," answered Laura, laughingly. "Let us start at once."

"Do you hear that, young person? She prefers me as I are! Now see what magic power her generosity has upon me!" And he darted into the tent, from which he issued in a moment with his Derby hat, a manzanita cane, a pocket handkerchief tied about his throat, and a flower pinned on his flannel camping-shirt, — a most ridiculous figure, since nothing seems so out of place in the woods as any suggestion of city costumes or customs. Laura was in high good-humor, and looked exceedingly brilliant and pretty, as she always did when she was the central figure of any group or the bright particular star of any occasion.

"Be home before dark," said Dr. Winship. "Pancho, keep a lookout for the pack-mule. Truth, one of the pack-mules has disappeared."

"So? Dumpling or Ditto?"

"Ditto, curiously enough. His name should have led him not to set an example, but to follow one."

Elsie came.

Perhaps you thought that this was going to be an exciting story, and that something would happen to keep her at the Tacitas ranch; but nothing did. Everything came to pass exactly as it was arranged, and Jack met his mother and sister at twelve o'clock some four miles from the camp, and escorted them to the gates.

"Welcome" had been painted on twenty different boards or bits of white cloth and paper, and nailed here and there on the trees that lined the rough wood-road; the strains of an orchestra, formed of a guitar, banjo, castanets, Chinese fiddle, and tin cans, greeted them from a distance, but were properly allowed to die away in silence when the guest neared the tents. Everything wore a new and smiling face, and Elsie never came more dangerously near being squeezed to death.

Elsie, in the prettiest of gingham dresses, and her cloud of golden hair braided in two funny little pugs to keep it out of the dust; Elsie, with a wide hat that shaded her face, already a little tanned and burned, no longer colorless; Elsie, with no lines of pain in her pretty forehead, and the hollow ring gone from her voice; Elsie, who jumped over the wheel of the wagon, and hugged her huggers with the strength of a young bear! It was too good to believe, and nobody did quite believe it for days.

At three o'clock, the happiest party in the

world assembled at the rough dining-table under the sycamore-trees.

Elsie beamed upon the feast from the high-backed manzanita chair, a faint color in her cheeks, and starry prisms of light in a pair of eyes that had not sparkled for many a weary month. Hop Yet smiled a trifle himself, wore his cap with a red button on the top to wait upon the table, and ministered to the hungry people with more interest and alacrity than he had shown since he had been dragged from Santa Barbara, his Joss, and his nightly game of fan-tan. And such a dinner as he had prepared in honor of the occasion! — longer by four courses than usual, and each person was allowed two plates in the course of the meal.

BILL OF FARE FOR HER MAJESTY'S DINNER.

Quail Soup.   Crackers.

Chili Colorado.

(Mutton stew, in Spanish style, with Chili peppers, tomatoes, and onions.)

Cold Boiled Ham.   Fried Potatoes.

Apples and Onions stewed together.

Gingersnaps.   Pickles.

Peaches, Apricots, and Nectarines.

California nuts and raisins.   Coffee.

And last of all, a surprise of Bell's, flapjacks,

long teased for by the boys, and prepared and fried by her own hands while the merry party waited at table, to get them smoking hot.

She came in flushed with heat and pride, the prettiest cook anybody ever saw, with her hair bobbed up out of the way and doing its best to escape, a high-necked white apron, sleeves rolled up to the elbow, and an insinuating spot of batter in the dimple of her left cheek.

" There ! " she cried, joyfully, as she deposited a heaping plate in front of her mother, and set the tin can of maple syrup by its side. " Begin on those, and I 'll fry like lightning on two griddles to keep up with you," and she rushed to the brush kitchen to turn her next installments that had been left to brown. Hop Yet had retired to a distant spot by the brook, and was washing dish-towels. All Chinese cooks are alike in their horror of a woman in the kitchen ; but some of them will unbend so far as to allow her to amuse herself so long as they are not required to witness the disagreeable spectacle.

Bell delicately inserted the cake-turner under the curled edges of the flapjacks and turned them over deftly, using a little too much force, perhaps, in the downward stroke when she flung them back on the griddle.

"Seems to me they come down with considerable of a thud," she said, reflectively. "I hope they're not tough, for I should never hear the last of it. Guess I'll punch one with the handle of this tin shovel, and see how it acts. Goodness! it's sort of — elastic. That's funny. Well, perhaps it's the way they ought to look." Here she transferred the smoking mysteries to her plate, passed a bit of pork over the griddles, and, after ladling out eight more, flew off to the group at the table.

"Are they good?" she was beginning to ask, when the words were frozen on her lips by the sight of a significant tableau.

The four boys were standing on the bench that served instead of dining-chairs, each with a plate and a pancake on the table in front of them. Jack held a hammer and spike, Scott Burton a hatchet, Geoffrey a saw, and Philip a rifle. Bell was nothing if not intuitive. No elaborate explanations ever were needed to show her a fact. Without a word she flung the plate of flapjacks she held as far into a thicket as she had force to fling it, and then dropped on her knees.

> "'Shoot, if you must, this old gray head,
> But spare my flapjacks, sirs,' she said!

"What's the matter with them? Tough?

I refuse to believe it. Your tools are too dull, — that's all. Use more energy! Nothing in this world can be accomplished without effort."

"They're a lovely brown," began Mrs. Winship, sympathetically.

"And they have a very good flavor," added Elsie.

"Don't touch them, dearest!" cried Bell, snatching the plate from under Elsie's very nose. "I won't have you made ill by my failures. But as for the boys, I don't care a fig for them. Let them make flapjacks more to their taste, the odious things! Polly Oliver, did you put in that baking powder, as I told you, while I went for the pork?"

Polly blanched. "Baking powder?" she faltered.

"Yes, baking powder! B–A–K–I–N–G P–O–W–D–E–R! Do I make myself plain?"

"Oh, baking powder, to be sure. Well, now that you mention the matter, I do remember that Dicky called me away just as I was getting it; and now that I think of it, Elsie came just afterwards, and — and" —

"And that's the whole of my story, O," sang Jack. "I recommend the criminal to the mercy of the court."

"A case of too many cooks," laughed Dr.

Winship. "Cheer up, girls; better fortune next time."

"There are eight more of them burning on the griddles this moment, Polly," said Bell, scathingly; "and as they are yours, not mine, I advise you to throw them in the brook, with the rest of the batter, so that Hop Yet won't know that there has been a failure."

"Some people blight everything they touch," sighed Polly, gloomily, as she departed for the kitchen.

"But when I lie in the green kirkyard" —

"Oh, Polly, dear," interrupted Margery, "that apology will not serve any longer; you 've used it too often."

"This is going to be entirely different," continued Polly, tragically.

"But when I lie in the green kirkyard,
With the mould upon my breast,
Say not that she made flapjacks well,
Only, she did her best."

"We promise!" cried Bell.

CHAPTER VII.

POLLY'S BIRTHDAY: FIRST HALF.

IN WHICH SHE REJOICES AT THE MERE FACT OF HER EXISTENCE.

"'O frabjous day! Calooh! Callay!'
He chortled in his joy."

POLLY'S birthday dawned auspiciously. At six o'clock she was kissed out of a sound sleep by Bell and Margery, and the three girls slipped on their wrappers, and prepared to run through the trees for a morning plunge in Mirror Pool. Although it was August there was still water enough in Minnehaha Brook to give one a refreshing dip. Mirror Pool was a quarter of a mile distant, and well guarded with rocks and deep hidden in trees; but a little pathway had been made to the water's edge, and thus the girls had easy access to what they called The Mermaid's Bath. A bay-tree was adorned with a little redwood sign, which bore a picture of a mermaid, drawn by Margery, and below the name these lines in rustic letters : —

> "A hidden brook,
> That to the sleeping woods all night
> Singeth a quiet tune."

Laura had not lived long enough in the woods to enjoy these cold plunges ; and, as her ideal was a marble tub, with scented water, and a French maid to apply the same with a velvet sponge, it is not much wonder. She insisted that, though it was doubtless a very romantic proceeding, the bottom and sides of the natural tub were quite too rocky and rough for her taste, and that she should be in constant terror of snakes curling round her toes.

"I 've a great mind to wake Laura, just for once," said Bell, opening the tent door. "There never was such a morning ! (I believe I 've said that regularly every day; but I simply never can get used to it.) There must have been a wonderful sunrise, dears, for the glow has n't faded yet. Not a bit of morning fog, — that 's good for Elsie. And what a lovely day for a birthday ! Did they use to give you anything like this in Vermont, Polly?"

"Hardly," said Polly, peering over Bell's shoulder. "Let's see. What did they give us in Vermont this month? Why, I can't think of anything but dog-days, hot nights, and hay fever; but that sounds ungrateful. Why, Geoff's up already! There's Elsie's bunch of vines, and twigs, and pretty things hanging on her tent-door. He's been off on horseback. Just my luck to have him get up first. Jack always does, you know; and last night I sewed up the tent-opening with carpet-thread, good and tight, overhand, — stitches I would n't be ashamed of at a sewing-school."

"Oh, you naughty girl!" laughed Bell. "The boys could rip it open with a knife in half the time it took you to sew it."

"Certainly. I did n't mean to keep them sewed up all day; but I thought I'd like Jack to remember me the first thing this morning."

"Girls," whispered Margery, excitedly, "don't stand there mooning — or sunning — forever! I thought there was a gopher in this tent last night. I heard something scratching, and I thought it was the dog outside; but just look at these two holes almost under Laura's pillow!"

"Let's fill them up, cover them over, anything!" gasped Bell. "Laura will never sleep here another night, if she sees them."

"Nobody insured Laura against gophers," said Polly. "She must take the fortunes of war."

"I would n't wake her," said Margery. "She did n't sleep well, and her face is flushed. Come, or we shall be late for breakfast."

When they returned, fresh and rosy, from their bath, there was a stir of life in all the tents. Pancho had come from the stage-station with mail; an odor of breakfast issued from the kitchen, where Hop Yet was humming a fragment of Chinese song, that ran something like this, — not loud, but unearthly enough, as Bell used to say, to spoil almost any cooking : —

Nasally.

Fong fong mong mong tiu he sun yi - u

sow chong how ki-u me yun tan-tar che ku choi song!

Dicky was abroad, radiant in a new suit of clothes, and Elsie pushed her golden head out between the curtains, and proclaimed herself strong enough for a wrestling-match with any boy or man about the camp.

But they found Laura sitting on the edge of her straw bed, directly over the concealed gopher-holes, a mirror in her hand and an expression of abject misery on her countenance.

"What's the matter?" cried the girls in one breath. But they needed no answer, as she turned her face towards the light, for it was plainly a case of poison-oak, — one eye almost closed, and the cheek scarlet and swollen.

"Where do you suppose you got it?" asked Bell.

"Oh, I don't know. It's everywhere; so I don't see how I ever hoped to escape it. Yet I've worn gloves every minute. I think I must have touched it when I went up the mountain trail with Jack. I'm a perfect fright already, and I suppose it has only begun."

"Is it very painful?" asked Polly, sympathetically. "Oh, you do look so funny, I can hardly help laughing, but I'm as sorry as I can be."

"I should expect you to laugh, — you generally do," retorted Laura. "No, it's not painful yet; but I don't care about that, — it's looking so ridiculous. I wonder if Dr. Winship could send me home. I wish now that I had gone with Scott, for I can't be penned up in this tent a week."

" Oh, it won't hurt you to go out," said Bell, " and you can lie in the sitting-room. Just wait, and let mamma try and cure you. She's a famous doctor." And Bell finished dressing hurriedly, and went to her mother's tent, while Polly and Margery smoothed the bed with a furtive kick of straw over the offending gopher-holes, and hung a dark shawl so as to shield Laura's eyes.

Aunt Truth entered speedily, with a family medical guide under one arm, and a box of remedies under the other.

" The doctor has told me just what to do, and he will see you after breakfast himself. It does n't look so very bad a case, dear ; don't run about in the sun for a day or two, and we 'll bring you out all right. The doctor has had us all under treatment at some time or other, because of that troublesome little plant."

" I don't want to get up to breakfast," moaned Laura.

" Just as you like. But it is Polly's birthday, you know (many happy returns, my sweet Pollykins), and there are great preparations going on."

" I can't help it, Mrs. Winship. The boys would make fun of my looks ; and I should n't blame them."

"Appear as the Veiled Lady," suggested Margery, as Mrs. Winship went out.

"I won't come, and that's the end of it," said Laura. "Perhaps if I bathe my face all the morning I can come to dinner."

After breakfast was cleared away, Hop Yet and Mrs. Howard's little China boy Gin were given a half holiday, and allowed to go to a neighboring ranch to see a "flend" of Hop Yet's; for it was a part of the birthday scheme that Bell and Geoffrey should cook the festival dinner.

Jack was so delighted at the failure of Polly's scheme to sew him in his tent that he simply radiated amiability, and spent the whole morning helping Elsie and Margery with a set of elaborate dinner-cards, executed on half sheets of note-paper.

The dinner itself was a grand success. Half of the cards bore a caricature of Polly in the shape of a parrot, with the inscription "Polly want a cracker?" The rest were adorned with pretty sketches of her in her camping-dress, a kettle in one hand, and underneath,

"Polly put the kettle on,
    We'll all have tea."

This was the bill of fare arranged by Bell and Geoffrey, and written on the reverse side of the dinner-cards : —

DINNER À LA MOTHER GOOSE.

CAMP CHAPARRAL.

August 15, 18—.

———

"Come with a whoop, come with a call ;
Come with a good will, or not at all."

———

"VICTUALS AND DRINK."

BEAN SOUP.

" She gave them some broth, she gave them some bread."

SALT CODFISH.

" You shall have a fishy
In a little dishy."

ROAST MUTTON À LA VENISON.

" Dear sensibility, O la !
I heard a little lamb cry ba-a ! "

POTATOES IN JACKETS.

" The butcher, the baker, the candlestick maker,
All jumped out of a roasted potato."

STEWED BEANS.

" You, nor I, nor nobody knows,
Where oats, peas, beans, and barley grows."

CHICKEN AND BEEF SANDWICHES.

" Hickety, pickety, my pretty hen
Laid good eggs for gentlemen."

" Taffy was a Welshman, Taffy was a thief,
Taffy came to my house and stole a piece of beef."

LEMON PIE.

" A pie sat on a pear-tree."

PLUM TARTS.

" The Queen of Hearts, she made some tarts,
All on a summer's day."

Fruit, Nuts, and Raisins.

" You shall have an apple,
  You shall have a plum."

" I had a little nut-tree, nothing would it bear
  But a silver nutmeg and a golden pear."

Bread and Cheese.

" When I was a bachelor I lived by myself,
  And all the bread and cheese I got I put upon the shelf."

Coffee and Lemonade.

" One, two, three, how good you be !
  I love coffee and Billy loves tea."

" Oranges and lemons,
  Says the bell of St. Clemen's."

" What they ate I can't tell,
  But 't is known very well
  That none of the party grew fat."

Bell and Geoff took turns at " dishing up " in
the kitchen, and sat down at the table between
whiles ; and they barely escaped being mobbed
when they omitted one or two dishes on the pro-
gramme, and confessed that they had been put
on principally for the " style " of the thing, —
a very poor excuse to a company of people who
have made up their mouths for all the delicacies
of the season.

Jack was head waiter, and having donned a
clean white blouse of Hop Yet's and his best
cap with the red button, from which dangled
a hastily improvised queue of black worsted,
he proceeded to convulse everybody with his

Mongolian antics. These consisted of most informal remarks in clever pigeon English, and snatches of Chinese melody, rendered from time to time as he carried dishes into the kitchen. Elsie laughed until she cried, and Laura sat in the shadiest corner, her head artistically swathed in white tarlatan.

Polly occupied the seat of honor at the end of the table opposite Dr. Winship, and was happier than a queen. She wore her new green cambric, with a bunch of leaves at her belt. She was sunburned, but the freckles seemed to have disappeared mysteriously from her nose, and almost any one would have admired the rosy skin, the dancing eyes, and the graceful little auburn head, " sunning over with curls."

When the last bit of dessert had been disposed of, and Dicky had gone to sleep in his mother's lap, like an infant boa-constrictor after a hearty meal, the presentation of gifts and reading of poems took place ; and Polly had to be on the alert to answer all the nonsensical jokes that were aimed at her.

Finally, Bell crowned the occasion by producing a song of Miss Mulock's, which had come in the morning mail from some girl friend of Polly's in the East, who had discovered that Polly's name had appeared in poetry and song without her knowledge, and who thought she might be interested to hear the composition. With the aid of Bell's guitar and Jack's banjo, the girls and boys soon caught the pretty air, and sung it in chorus.

1. Pret-ty Pol-ly Ol-i-ver, will you be my own?
2. Pret-ty Pol-ly Ol-i-ver, I love you so dear!
3. Pret-ty Pol-ly Ol-i-ver, I'll bid you good bye:

Pret-ty Pol-ly Ol-i-ver, as cold as a
Pret-ty Pol-ly Ol-i-ver, my hope and my
Pret-ty Pol-ly Ol-i-ver, for you I'll not

stone; But my love has grown warm-er as
fear; I've wait-ed for you, sweet-heart, this
die; You'll nev-er get a tru-er true

cold-er you've grown, O Pret-ty Pol-ly
many a long year; For Pret-ty Pol-ly
lov-er than I, So Pret-ty Pol-ly

Ol-i-ver, will you be my own?
Ol-i-ver, I've loved you so dear!
Ol-i-ver, good-bye, love, good-bye!

At the end, Dr. Winship raised his glass of lemonade, and proposed to drink Miss Oliver's health. This was done with enthusiasm, and Geoffrey immediately cried, "Speech, speech!"

"I can't," said Polly, blushing furiously.

"Speech!" sung Jack and Philip vociferously, pounding on the table with knife-handles to increase the furore.

"Speech!" demanded the genial doctor, going over to the majority, and smiling encouragingly at Polly, who was pushed to her feet before she knew very well what she was doing. "Oh, if Laura were not looking at me," she thought, "I'd just like to speak right out, and tell them a little bit of what is in my heart. I don't care — I will!"

"I know you are all in fun," she said, looking bravely into the good doctor's eyes, "and of course no one could make a proper speech with Jack grinning like a Cheshire cat, but I can't help telling you that this is the happiest summer and the happiest birthday of my whole life, and that I scarcely remember nowadays that I have no father and no brothers and sisters, for I have never been alone or unhappy since you took me in among you and Bell chose me for her friend; and I think that if you knew how grateful I am for my beautiful summer, dear Dr. Paul and aunt Truth, you would be glad that you gave it to me, and I love you all, dearly, dearly, dearly!" Whereupon the impulsive little creature finished her maiden speech by dashing round the table and giving Mrs. Winship one of her "bear hugs," at which everybody laughed and rose from the table.

Laura Burton, who was thoroughly out of conceit with the world, and who was never quite happy when other people seemed for the moment to be preferred to herself, thought this burst of affection decidedly theatrical, but she did not know of any one to whom she could confide her opinions just then; indeed, she felt too depressed and out of sorts to join in the general hilarity.

Dinner being over, Dr. Paul and the boys took the children and sauntered up the cañon for a lazy afternoon with their books. Elsie went to sleep in the new hammock that the doctor had hung in the sycamores back of the girls' sleeping-tent, and Mrs. Winship lay down for her afternoon nap. Pancho saddled the horses for Bell and Margery, who went for a gallop. Polly climbed into the sky-parlor to write a long letter to her mother, and Laura was left to solitude in the sleeping-tent. Now everybody knows that a tent at midday is not a particularly pleasant spot, and after many a groan at the glare of the sun, which could not be tempered by any system of shawls, and moans at the gopher-holes which she discovered while searching for her ear-ring, and repeated consultations with the hand-glass at brief intervals, during which she convinced herself that she looked worse every minute, she finally discovered a series of alarming new spots on her neck and chin. She felt then that camping out was a complete failure, and that she would be taken home forthwith if it could be managed, since she saw nothing before her but day after day of close confinement and unattractive personal appearance. "It's just my luck!" she grumbled, as she twisted up her hair and made herself as presentable as possible under the trying circumstances. "I don't think I ever had a becoming or an interesting illness. The chicken-pox, mumps, and sties on my eyes, — that's the sort of thing I have!"

"I feel much worse, Mrs. Winship," she said, going into the sitting-room tent and waking aunt Truth from a peaceful snooze. "If you can spare Pancho over night, I really think I must trouble you to send Anne and me home at once. I feel as if I wanted to go to bed in a dark room, and I shall only be a bother if I stay."

"Why, my child, I'm sorry to have you go

off with your visit unfinished. You know we don't mind any amount of trouble, if we can make you comfortable."

"You are very kind, but indeed I'd rather go."

"I hardly dare let you start in the hot sun without consulting the doctor, and everybody is away except Polly; they will feel badly not to say good-by."

"It is nearly three o'clock now, so the worst of the sun is over, and we shall be at the ranch by eight this evening. I feel too ill to say good-by, any way, and we shall meet Bell and Margery somewhere on the road, for they were going to the milk ranch."

"Very well, my dear, if you've made up your mind I must yield," replied Mrs. Winship, getting up and smoothing her hair. "I don't dare wake Elsie, she has had such an exciting day; but I'll call Polly to help you pack, and then tell Pancho to find Anne and harness the team. While he is doing that, I'll get you a little lunch to take with you and write a note to your mother. Perhaps you can come again before we break camp, but I'm sorry to send you home in such a sad plight."

CHAPTER VIII.

POLLY'S BIRTHDAY: SECOND HALF.

IN WHICH SHE WISHES SHE HAD NEVER BEEN BORN.

"From Hebrew wit the maxim sprung,
  Though feet should slip, ne'er let the tongue."

POLLY came at once to the tent, where she
found Laura getting her belongings together.

"Why, Laura, it seems too bad you should
go off so suddenly. What can I do to help
you?"

The very spirit of evil entered Laura's heart
as she looked at Polly, so fresh and pretty and
radiant, with her dimples dancing in and out,

her hair ruffled with the effort of literary composition, and the glow of the day's happiness still shining in her eyes. She felt as if Polly was " glad inside " that she was poisoned; she felt sure she was internally jumping for joy at her departure; and above all, she felt that Polly was entirely too conceited over the attention she had received that day, and needed to be " taken down a peg or two." " Red-haired, stuck-up, saucy thing," she thought, " how I should like to give her a piece of my mind before I leave this place, if I only dared!" " I don't need any help, thank you," she said aloud, in her iciest manner.

" But it will only make your head ache to bend over and tug away at that valise, and I 'll be only too glad to do it."

" I 've no doubt of that," responded Laura, meaningly. " It is useless for you to make any show of regret over my going, for I know perfectly well that you are glad to get me out of the way."

" Why, Laura, what do you mean?" exclaimed Polly, completely dazed at this bombshell of candor.

" I mean what I say; and I should have said it before if I could ever have found a chance. Because I did n't mention it at the time, you need n't suppose I 've forgotten your getting me into trouble with Mrs. Winship, the day before the Howards came."

" That was not my fault," said Polly, hotly. " I did n't speak any louder than the other girls, and I did n't know aunt Truth objected to Mrs. Pinkerton, and I did n't know she was anywhere near."

" You roared like the bull of Bashan, — that 's what you did. Perhaps you can't help your voice, but anybody in the cañon could have heard you ; and Mrs. Winship has n't been the same to me since, and the boys don't take the slightest notice of me lately."

" You are entirely mistaken, Laura. Dr. and Mrs. Winship are just as lovely and cordial to you as they are to everybody else, and the boys do not feel well enough acquainted with you to ' frolic ' with you as they do with us."

" It is n't so, but you are not sensitive enough to see it ; and I should never have been poisoned if it had n't been for you ! "

" Oh, go on, do ! " said Polly, beginning to lose her self-control, which was never very great. " I did n't know I was a Lucrezia Borgia in disguise. How did I poison you, pray ? "

" I did n't say you poisoned me ; but you made me so uncomfortable that day, bringing down

Mrs. Winship's lecture on my head and getting my best friend abused, that I was glad to get away from the camp, and went out with Jack for that reason when I was too tired and warm; and you are always trying to cut me out with Bell and the boys."

"That's a perfectly — jet black — fib!" cried Polly, who was now thoroughly angry; "and I don't think it is very polite of you to attack the whole party, and say they haven't been nice to you, when they've done everything in the world!"

"It isn't your party any more than mine, is it? And if I don't know how to be polite, I certainly sha'n't ask *you* for instruction; for I must know as much about the manners of good society as you do, inasmuch as I have certainly seen more of it!"

Polly sank into a camp-chair, too stunned for a moment to reply, while Laura, who had gone quite beyond the point where she knew or cared what she said, went on with a rush of words: "I mean to tell you, now that I am started, that anybody who isn't blind can see why you toady to the Winships, who have money and social position, and why you are so anxious to keep everybody else from getting into their good graces; but they are so par-

tial to you that they have given you an entirely
false idea of yourself; and you might as well
know that unless you keep yourself a little more
in the background, and grow a little less bold
and affected and independent, other people will
not be quite as ready as the Winships to make
a pet of a girl whose mother keeps a boarding-
house."

Poor Laura! It was no sooner said than
she regretted it, — a little, not much. But
poor Polly! Where was her good angel then?
Why could she not have treated this thrust
with the silence and contempt it deserved?
But how could Laura have detected and probed
the most sensitive spot in the girl's nature?
She lost all command of herself. Her rage
absolutely frightened her, for it made her deaf
and blind to all considerations of propriety and
self-respect, and for a moment she was only
conscious of the wild desire to strike — yes,
even to kill — the person who had so insulted
all that was dearest to her.

"Don't dare to say another word!" she
panted, with such flaming cheeks and such
flashing eyes that Laura involuntarily retreated
towards the door, half afraid of the tempest her
words had evoked. "Don't dare to say another
word, or I don't know what I may do! Yes,

I am glad you are going, and everybody will be glad, and the sooner you go the better! You 've made everybody miserable ever since you came, with your jealousy and your gossip and your fine-lady airs; and if aunt Truth had n't loved your mother, and if we were mean enough to tell tales, we would have repeated some of your disagreeable speeches long ago. How can you dare to say I love the Winships for anything but themselves? And if you had ever seen my darling mother, you never could have called her a boarding-house keeper, you cruel " —

Oh, but the dashing torrent of angry words stopped at the mere mention of her mother. The word recalled her to herself, but too late. It woke in her memory the clasp of her mother's arms, the sound of the sweet, tired voice : " Only two of us against the big world, Polly, — you and I. Be brave, little daughter, brave and patient." Oh, how impatient and cowardly she had been! Would she never learn to be good? The better impulses rushed back into her heart, and crowded out the bad ones so quickly that in another moment she would have flung herself at Laura's feet, and implored her forgiveness merely to gain again her own self-respect and her mother's approval; but there was no time for repentance (there is n't, sometimes), for the clatter of wheels announced Pancho's approach with the team, and Mrs. Winship and Anne Burton came into view, walking rapidly towards the tent.

Laura was a good deal disconcerted at their ill-timed appearance, but reflected rapidly that if Mrs. Winship had overheard anything, it was probably Polly's last speech, in which case that young person would seem to be more in fault than herself, so stepping out of the tent she met Mrs. Winship and kissed her good-by.

Little Anne ran on and jumped into the wagon, with all a child's joy at the prospect of going anywhere. Polly's back was turned, but she could not disappear entirely within the tent without causing Mrs. Winship surprise; and she went through a lifetime of misery and self-reproach in that minute of shame and fear, when she dared neither to advance nor retreat.

"I don't quite like to let you go alone, Laura, without consulting the doctor, and I can't find him," said Mrs. Winship. "Why, you are nervous and trembling! Had n't you better wait until to-morrow?"

"No, thank you, Mrs. Winship. I am all ready now, and would prefer to go. I think perhaps I have stayed quite long enough, as

Polly has just told me that everybody is glad to see the last of me, and that I 've made you all miserable since I came."

This was the climax to Polly's misery; for she was already so overcome by the thought of her rudeness that she was on the point of begging Laura's pardon for that particular speech then and there, and she had only to hear her exact words repeated to feel how they would sound in Mrs. Winship's ears.

Mrs. Winship was so entirely taken aback by Laura's remark, that she could only ejaculate, " Polly — said — that ! What do you mean ? "

" Oh, I am quite ready to think she said more than she intended, but those were her words."

" Polly ! "

Polly turned. Alas! it was plain enough that this was no false accusation. Her downcast eyes, flushed, tear-stained cheeks, quivering lips, and the silent shame of her whole figure spoke too clearly.

" Can it be possible, Polly, that you spoke in such a way to a guest who was about to leave my house? "

" Yes."

The word was wrung from Polly's trembling

lips. What could she say but " Yes," — it was
true, — and how could she repeat the taunts
that had provoked her to retort? They were
not a sufficient excuse ; and for that matter,
nothing could be a sufficient excuse for her language. Now that she was confronted with her
own fault, Laura's seemed so small beside it that
she would have been ashamed to offer it as any
justification.

Mrs. Winship grew pale, and for a moment
was quite at a loss as to the treatment of such
a situation.

"Don't say any more about it, Mrs. Winship," said Laura ; "we were both angry, or
we should never have forgotten ourselves, and
I shall think no more of it." Laura spoke
with such an air of modest virtue, and seemed
so ready to forgive and forget, that Polly in
her silence and confusion appeared worse than
ever.

"But I want you to remember that you are
my guest, not Pauline's ; that I asked you to
come and ask you to remain. I cannot allow
you to go simply because you do not chance
to be a favorite with another of my guests."
(Oh ! the pang these words gave Polly's faulty,
tender little heart !)

"I am only going because I feel so ill, —

not a bit because of what Polly said; I was in the wrong too, perhaps, but I promise not to let anybody nor anything make me quarrel when I visit you again. Good-by!" and Laura stepped into the wagon.

"I trust you will not mention this to your mother, since I hope it is the only unpleasant incident of your visit; and it is no fault of mine that you go away with an unhappy impression of our hospitality." Here Mrs. Winship reached up and kissed little Anne, and as the horses were restive, and no one seemed to have anything further to say, Pancho drove off.

"I don't care to talk with you any more at present, Polly," said Mrs. Winship. "I am too hurt and too indignant to speak of your conduct quietly. I know the struggles you have with your temper, and I am quite willing to sympathize with you even when you do not come off victorious; but this is something quite different. I can't conceive how any amount of provocation or dislike could have led you into such disloyalty to me;" and with this she walked away.

Polly staggered into a little play-room tent of Dicky's, where she knew that she could be alone, pinned the curtains together so that no one could peep in, and threw herself down upon the long cushioned seat where Dicky was wont to take his afternoon nap. There, in grief and despair, she sobbed the afternoon through, dreading to be disturbed and dreading to be questioned.

"My beautiful birthday spoiled," she moaned, "and all my own fault! I was so happy this morning, but now was ever anybody so miserable as I! And even if I tell aunt Truth what Laura said, she will think it no excuse, and it is n't!"

As it neared supper-time she made an opening in the back of the tent, and after long watching caught sight of Gin on his way to the brook for water, signaled him, and gave him this despairing little note for Mrs. Winship.

DEAR AUNT TRUTH, — I don't ask you to forgive me, — I don't deserve to be forgiven, — but I ask you to do me just one more of your dear little kindnesses. Let me stay alone in Dicky's tent till morning, and please don't let any one come near me. You can tell everybody the whole story to-night, if you think best, though I should be glad if only Dr. Paul and Bell need know; but I do not mind anything after displeasing you, — nothing can be so bad

as that. Perhaps you think I ought to come
out and confess it to them myself, as a pun-
ishment; but oh, aunt Truth, I am punishing
myself in here alone worse than any one else
can do it. I will go back to Santa Barbara
any time that you can send me to the stage
station, and I will never ask you to love me
again until I have learned how to control my
temper.   Your wretched, wretched

POLLY.

P. S. I remember that it is my birthday,
and all that you have done for me, to-day
and all the other days. It looks as if I were
ungrateful, but in spite of what I did I am not.
The words just blazed out, and I never knew
that they were going to be said till I heard
them falling from my mouth. It seems to me
that if I ever atone for this I will have a slate
and pencil hanging to my belt, and only write
what I have to say.   POLLY.

The moisture came to Mrs. Winship's eyes
as she read this tear-stained little note.
"There's something here I don't quite understand," she thought; "and yet Polly confessed
that Laura told the truth. Poor child! — but
she has got to learn patience and self-control
through suffering. However, I'll keep the

matter a secret from everybody at present, and stand between her and my inquisitive brood of youngsters," and she slipped the note into her pocket.

At six o'clock the members of the family came into camp from various directions, and gathered about the supper-table. All were surprised at Laura's sudden departure, but no one seemed especially grief-stricken. Dicky announced confidentially to Philip that Laura was a "norful 'fraid-cat of frogs," and Jack ventured the opinion that Miss Laura had n't "boy" enough in her for camp-life.

"But where is Polly?" asked Bell, looking round the table, as she pinned up her riding-skirt and sat down in her usual seat.

"She has a bad headache, and is lying down," said Mrs. Winship quietly; "she 'll be all right in the morning."

"Headache!" ejaculated four or five people at once, dropping their napkins and looking at each other in dismay.

"I 'll go and rub her head with cologne," said Margery.

"Let me go and sit with her," said Elsie.

"Have you been teasing her, Jack?" asked Mrs. Howard.

"Too much birthday?" asked Dr. Paul.

"Tell her we can spare almost anybody else better."

"Bless the child, she wants *me* if she is sick. Go on with your suppers, I'll see to her," and Bell rose from the table.

"No, my dear, I want you all to leave her alone at present," said Mrs. Winship, decidedly. "I've put her to bed in Dicky's play-tent, and I want her to be quiet. Gin has taken her some supper, and she needs rest."

Polly Oliver in need of rest! What an incomprehensible statement! Nobody was satisfied, but there was nothing more to be said, though Bell and Philip exchanged glances as much as to say, "Something is wrong."

Supper ended, and they gathered round the camp-fire, but nothing was quite as usual. It was all very well to crack jokes, but where was a certain merry laugh that was wont to ring out, at the smallest provocation, in such an infectious way that everybody else followed suit? And who was there, when Polly had the headache, to make a saucy speech and look down into the fire innocently, while her dimples did everything that was required in order to point the shaft? And pray what was the use of singing when there was no alto to Bell's treble, or of giving conundrums, since it was always

Polly who thought of nonsensical answers better than the real ones? And as for Jack, why, it was folly to shoot arrows of wit into the air when there was no target. He simply stretched himself out beside Elsie, who was particularly quiet and snoozed peacefully, without taking any part in the conversation, avowing his intention to "turn in" early. "Turn in" early, forsooth! What was the matter with the boy?

"It's no use," said Bell, plaintively, "we can't be anything but happy, now that we have Elsie here; but it needs only one small headache to show that Polly fills a long-felt want in this camp. You think of her as a modest spoke in the wheel till she disappears, and then you find she was the hub."

"Yes," said Margery, "I think every one round this fire is simply angelic, unless I except Jack, but the fact is that Polly is — well, she is — Polly, and I dare any one to contradict me."

"The judgment of the court is confirmed,' said Philip.

> "And the shark said, 'If you
> Don't believe it is true,
> Just look at my wisdom tooth!'"

sang Geoffrey.

" And if any one ever tells me again that she has red hair and has n't good features, I should just like to show them a picture of her as she was to-day at the dinner table! " exclaimed Bell.

" As if anybody needed features with those dimples," added Elsie, " or would mind red hair when it was such pretty hair! "

" I think a report of this conversation would go far towards curing Polly," said Dr. Winship, with a smile.

" And you say we can't go in there before we go to bed, *mamacita?* " whispered Bell in her mother's ear, as the boys said good-night and went towards their tent.

" My dear," she answered decidedly, with a fond kiss for each of the girls, " Polly herself asked me to keep everybody away."

Polly herself wanted to be alone! Would wonders never cease?

Meanwhile Dicky, who had disappeared for a moment, came back to the fire, his bosom heaving with grief and rage.

" I went to my play-tent," he sobbed, " and putted my hand underneath the curtain and gave Polly a piece of my supper cake I saved for her — not the frosted part, but the burnt part I could n't eat — and she liked it and kissed my hand — and then I fought she was lonesome, and would like to see my littlest frog, and I told her to put out her hand again for a s'prise, and I squeezed him into it tight, so 't he would n't jump — and she fought it was more cake, and when she found it was n't she frew my littlest frog clear away, and it got losted!"

This brought a howl of mirth from everybody, and Dicky was instructed, while being put to bed, not to squeeze little frogs into people's hands in the dark, as it sometimes affected them unpleasantly.

All this time Polly was lying in the tent, quite exhausted with crying, and made more wretched by every sound of voices wafted towards her. Presently Gin appeared with her night wrapper and various things for comfort sent her by the girls; and as she wearily undressed herself and prepared for the night, she found three little messages of comfort pinned on the neck and sleeves of her flannel gown, written in such colossal letters that she could easily read them by the moonlight.

On the right sleeve: —

Cheer up! "I will never desert Mr. Micawber!" BELL.

On the left sleeve : —

DARLING POLLY, — Get well soon, or we shall all be sick in order to stay with you.

Lovingly,   MEG.

P. S. Jack said you were the *life of the camp!* What do you think of that ? ?   M.

On the neck : —

DEAREST, — You have always called me the Fairy Godmother, and pretended I could see things that other people could n't.

The boys (great stupids !) think you have the headache. We girls can all see that you are in trouble, but only the Fairy Godmother *knows why;* and though she can't make a beautiful gold coach out of this pumpkin, because there 's something wrong about the pumpkin, yet she will do her best for

Cinderella, and pull her out of the ashes somehow.

ELSIE.

Polly's tears fell fast on the dear little notes, which she kissed again and again, and tucked under her pillow to bring her sleep. " Elsie knows something," she thought, " but how? she knows that I'm in trouble and that I've done wrong, or she would n't have said that about not being able to turn a bad pumpkin into a beautiful gold coach; but perhaps she can get aunt Truth to forgive me and try me again. Unless she can do it, it will never come to pass, for I have n't the courage to ask her. I would rather run away early in the morning and go home than have her look at me again as she did to-day. Oh! what shall I do!" and Polly went down on her knees beside the rough couch, and sobbed her heart out in a childish prayer for help and comfort. It was just the prayer of a little child telling a sorrowful story; because it is when we are alone and in trouble that the unknown and mysterious God seems to us most like a Father, and we throw ourselves into the arms of his love like helpless children, and tell Him our secret thoughts and griefs.

" Dear Father in heaven," she sobbed,

"don't forgive me if I ought not to be forgiven, but please make aunt Truth feel how sorry I am, and show me whether I ought to tell what made me so angry, though it's no excuse. Bless and keep my darling patient little mother, and help me to grow more like her, and braver and stronger too, so that I can take care of her soon, and she need n't work hard any longer. Please forgive me for hating some things in my life as much as I do, and I will try and like them better; but I think — yes, I know — that I am full of wicked pride; and oh, it seems as if I could never, never get over wanting to live in a pretty house, and wear pretty dresses, and have my mother live like Bell's and Margery's. And oh, if Thou canst only forgive me for hating boarders so dreadfully and being ashamed of them every minute, I will try and like them better and tell everybody that we take them, — I will indeed; and if I can only once make aunt Truth love and trust me again, I will make the boarders' beds and dust their rooms forever without grumbling. Please, dear Father in heaven, remember that I have n't any father to love me or to teach me to be good; and though mamma does her best, please help her to make something out of me if it can be done. Amen."

" Truth," said Mrs. Howard, when all was quiet about the camp, " Elsie wants to see you a moment before she goes to sleep. Will you go to her tent, while I play a game of cribbage with Dr. Paul?"

Elsie looked like a blossom in all the beautiful greenness of her tent, with her yellow head coming out from above the greens and browns of the cretonne bed-cover for all the world like a daffodil pushing its way up through the mould towards the spring sunshine.

" Aunt Truth," she said softly, as Mrs. Winship sat down beside her, " you remember that Dr. Paul hung my hammock in a new place to-day, just behind the girls' sleeping-tent. Now I know that Polly is in trouble, and that you are displeased with her. What I want to ask, if I may, is, how much you know; for I overheard a great deal myself, — enough to feel that Polly deserves a hearing."

" I overheard nothing," replied Mrs. Winship. " All that I know Polly herself confessed in Laura's presence. Polly told Laura, just as she was going away, that everybody would be glad to see the last of her, and that she had made everybody miserable from the beginning of her visit. It was quite inexcusable, you know, dear, for one of my guests to waylay another, just as she was leaving, and make such a cruel speech. I would rather anything else had happened. I know how impetuous Polly is, and I can forgive the child almost anything, her heart is so full of love and generosity; but I cannot overlook such a breach of propriety as that. Of course I have seen that Laura is not a favorite with any of you. I confess she is not a very lovable person, and I think she has led a very unwholesome life lately and is sadly spoiled by it; still, that is no excuse for Polly's conduct."

"No, of course it isn't," sighed Elsie, with a little quiver of the lip. "I thought I could plead a better case for Polly, but I see exactly how thoughtless and impolite she was; yet, if you knew everything, auntie, dear, you would feel a little different. Do you think it was nice of Laura to repeat what Polly said right before her, and just as she was going away, when she knew it would make you uncomfortable and that you were not to blame for it?"

"No, hardly. It didn't show much tact; but girls of fifteen or sixteen are not always remarkable for social tact. I excused her partly because she was half sick and nervous."

"Well," Elsie went on, "I didn't hear the whole quarrel, so that I do not know how long

it lasted nor who began it. I can't help thinking it was Laura, though, for she's been trying
her best to provoke Polly for the last fortnight,
and until to-day she has never really succeeded.
I was half asleep, and heard at first only the
faint murmur of voices, but when I was fully
awake, Laura was telling Polly that she doted
on you simply because you had money and position, while she had not; that you were all so
partial to her that she had lost sight of her
own deficiencies. Then she called her bold and
affected, and I don't know what else, and finally
wound up by saying that nobody but the Winships would be likely to make a pet of the
daughter of a boarding-house keeper."

"Elsie!" ejaculated Mrs. Winship; "this
grows worse and worse! Is it possible that
Laura Burton could be guilty of such a
thought?"

"I can't be mistaken. I was too excited not
to hear very clearly; and the moment the words
were spoken I knew my poor dear's fiery temper would never endure that. And it did n't;
it blazed out in a second, but it did n't last
long, for before I could get to the tent she
had stopped herself right in the middle of
a sentence; and in another minute I heard
your voice, and crept back to the hammock,

thinking that everything would be settled by Laura's going away. I'd no idea that she would pounce on Polly and get her in disgrace, the very last thing, when she knew that she was responsible for the whole matter. You see, auntie, that, impolite as Polly was, she only told Laura that we girls were glad she was going. She did n't bring you in, after all ; and Laura knew perfectly well that she was a welcome visitor, and we all treated her with the greatest politeness, though it 's no use to say we liked her much."

"I am very sorry for the whole affair," sighed Mrs. Winship, " there is so much wrong on both sides. Laura's remark, it is true, would have angered almost anybody who was not old and wise enough to see that it deserved only contempt ; but both the girls should have had too much respect for themselves and for me to descend to such an unladylike quarrel. However, I am only too glad to hear anything which makes Polly's fault less, for I love her too dearly not to suffer when I have to be severe with her."

" She would n't ask you to overlook her fault," continued Elsie, with tears in her eyes. " I know just how wretched and penitent she must be, — Polly is always so fierce against her own faults, — but what must be making her suffer most is the thought that she has entirely lost your confidence and good opinion. Oh, I can't help thinking that God feels sorrier this very minute for Polly, who fights and fights against her temper, like a dear sunbeam trying to shine again and again when a cloud keeps covering it up, than He does for Laura, who has everything made smooth for her, and who is unhappy when her feathers are ruffled the least bit."

"You are right, dear, in so far that a fiery little soul like Polly's can, if it finds the right channels, do God's work in the world better than a character like Laura's, which is not courageous, nor strong, nor sweet enough for great service, unless it grows into better things through bitter or rich experiences. Now, good-night, my blessed little peacemaker; sleep sweetly, for I am going into Polly's tent to have a good talk with her."

As Mrs. Winship dropped the curtains of Elsie's tent behind her, and made her way quietly through the trees, the tinkling sound of a banjo fell upon the still night air; and presently, as she neared Polly's retreat, this facetious serenade, sung by Jack's well-known voice, was wafted to her ears : —

" Prithee, Polly Oliver, why bide ye so still?
    Pretty Polly Oliver, we fear you are ill.
    I'm singing 'neath thy window, when night dews are
        chill,
    For, pretty Polly Oliver, we hear you are ill."

She was about to dispatch Master Jack to
his tent with a round scolding, when the last
words of the song were frozen on his lips by
the sound of a smothered sob, in place of the
saucy retort he hoped to provoke. The unexpected sob frightened him more than any fusi-
lade of hot words, and he stole away in the
darkness more crestfallen than he had been for
many a year.

Mrs. Winship, more troubled than ever,
pulled apart the canvas curtains, and stood in
the opening, silently. The sight of the forlorn
little figure, huddled together on the straw bed,
touched her heart, and, when Polly started up
with an eloquent cry and flew into her extended
arms, she granted willing forgiveness, and the
history of the afternoon was sobbed out upon
her motherly shoulder.

The next morning Mrs. Winship announced
that Polly was better, sent breakfast to her tent,
and by skillful generalship drove everybody
away from the camp but Elsie, who brought
Polly to the sitting-room, made her comfortable
on the lounge, and, administering much good

advice to Margery and Bell concerning topics
to be avoided, admitted them one by one into
her presence, so that she gradually regained her
self-control. And at the dinner table a very
pale Polly was present again, with such a
white face and heavy eyes that no one could
doubt there had been a headache, while two
people, at least, knew that there had been a
heartache as well. The next day's mail carried the following letter to Laura Burton : —

CAMP CHAPARRAL, *August* 16, 188—.

MY DEAR LAURA, — As I told you when
you were leaving, I cannot well say how sorry
I am that anything should have occurred to
mar your pleasant remembrance of your stay
with us. That your dear mother's daughter
should have been treated with discourtesy while
she was my guest was very disagreeable to me ;
but I have learned that you were yourself
somewhat to blame in the affair, and therefore
you should have borne the harsh treatment you
received with considerable patience, and perhaps
have kept it quite to yourself. ("That little
cat told her, after all," said Laura, when she
read this. "I did n't think she was that kind.")
Polly would never have confessed the cause
of the quarrel, because she knew nothing could

justify her language; but Elsie was lying in the hammock behind the tent and overheard the remark which so roused Polly's anger. You were not aware, of course, how sore a spot you touched upon, or you could never have spoken as you did, though I well know that you were both too angry to reflect. Polly is a peculiarly proud and high-spirited girl, — proud, I confess, to a fault; but she comes, on her mother's side, from a long line of people who have had much to be proud of in the way of unblemished honesty, nobility, fine attainments, and splendid achievements. Of her father's honorable services to his country, and his sad and untimely death, you may have heard; but you may not know that Mrs. Oliver's misfortunes have been very many and very bitter, and that the only possibility of supporting and educating Polly lies at present in her taking boarders, for her health will not admit just now of her living anywhere save in Southern California. I fail to see why this is not thoroughly praiseworthy and respectable; but if you do not consider it quite an elegant occupation, I can only say that Mrs. Oliver presides over the table at which her "boarders" sit with a high-bred dignity and grace of manner that the highest lady in the land might imitate; and that, when health and circumstances permit her to diminish the distance between herself and the great world, she and her daughter Polly, by reason of their birth and their culture, will find doors swinging wide to admit them where you and I would find it difficult to enter. Polly apologizes sincerely for her rudeness, and will write you to that effect, as of course she does not know of this letter.

Sincerely your friend,

TRUTH WINSHIP.

CHAPTER IX.

ROUND THE CAMP-FIRE.

"The time before the fire they sat,
And shortened the delay by pleasing chat."

THE August days had slipped away one after another, and September was at hand. There was no perceptible change of weather to mark the advent of the new month. The hills were a little browner, the dust a little deeper, the fleas a little nimbler, and the water in the brook a trifle lower, but otherwise Dame Nature did not concern herself with the change of seasons, inasmuch as she had no old dresses to get rid of, and no new ones to put on for a long time yet; indeed, she is never very fashionable in this locality, and wears very much the same garments throughout the year.

Elsie seemed almost as strong as any of the

other girls now, and could enter with zest into
all their amusements. The appetite of a young
bear, the sound dreamless sleep of a baby, and
the constant breathing in of the pure, life-giv-
ing air had made her a new creature. Mrs.
Howard and Jack felt, day by day, that a burden of dread was being lifted from their hearts;
and Mrs. Howard especially felt that she loved
every rock and tree in the cañon.

It was a charming morning, and Polly was
seated at the dining-room table, deep in the
preparation of a lesson in reading and pro-
nunciation for Hop Yet. Her forehead was
creased with many wrinkles of thought, and she
bit the end of her lead-pencil as if she were
engaged in solving some difficult problem; but
if that were so, why did the dimples chase each
other in and out of her cheeks in such a sus-
picious fashion? She was a very gentle, a
very sedate Polly, these latter days, and not
only astonished her friends, but surprised herself, by her good behavior, her elegant reserve
of manner, her patience with Jack, and her
abject devotion to Dicky.

"I'm afraid it won't last," she sighed to
herself occasionally. "I'm almost too good.
That's always the way with me, — I must
either be so bad that everybody is discouraged,

or else so good that I frighten them. Now I catch Bell and Elsie exchanging glances every day, as much as to say, 'Poor Polly, she will never hold out at this rate; do you notice that nothing ruffles her, — that she is simply angelic?' As if I could n't be angelic for a fortnight! Why I have often done it for four weeks at a stretch!"

Margery was in the habit of giving Hop Yet an English lesson every other day, as he had been very loath to leave his evening school in Santa Barbara and bury himself in a cañon, away from all educational influences; but she had deserted her post for once and gone to ride with Elsie, so that Polly had taken her place and was evolving an exercise that Hop Yet would remember to the latest day of his life. It looked simple enough : —

1. The grass is dry.
2. The fruit is ripe.
3. The chaparral is green.
4. The new road is all right.
5. The bay-"rum" tree is fresh and pretty.

But as no Chinaman can pronounce the letter "r," it was laboriously rendered thus, when the unhappy time of the lesson came : —

1. The-glass-is-dly.
2. The-fluit-is-lipe.

3. The-chap-lal-is-gleen.

4. The-new-load-is-all-light-ee.

5. The bay-lum-tlee-is-flesh-and-plitty.

Finally, when she attempted to introduce the sentence, "Around the rough and rugged rock the ragged rascal ran," Hop Yet rose hurriedly, remarking, "All lightee : I go no more school jus' now. I lun get lunchee."

Bell came running down the path just then, and linking her arm in Polly's said, "Papa has the nicest plan. You know the boys are so disappointed that Colonel Jackson did n't ask them over to that *rodeo* at his cattle ranch, — though a summer *rodeo* is only to sort out fat cattle to sell, and it is not very exciting ; but papa promised to tell them all about the old-fashioned kind some night, and he has just remembered that to-morrow is Admission Day, September 9, so he proposes a real celebration round the camp-fire to amuse Elsie. She does n't know anything about California even as it is now, and none of us know what it was in the old days. Don't you think it will be fun ? "

" Perfectly splendid ! "

" And papa wants us each to contribute something."

" A picnic ! — but I don't know anything."

"That's just what I'm coming to. I have such a bright idea. He said that we might look in any of his books, but Geoff and Jack are at them already, and I'd like a surprise. Now Juan Capistrano, an old vaquero of Colonel Jackson's, is over here. He is a wonderful rider; papa says that he could ride on a comet, if he could get a chance to mount. It was he who told the boys that the *rodeo* was over. Now I propose that we go and interview Pancho and Juan, and get them to tell us some old California stories. They are both as stupid as they can be, but they must have had some adventures, I suppose, somewhere, sometime. I'll translate and write the things down, for my part, and you and Margery can tell them."

"Lovely! Oh, if we can only get an exciting grizzly story, so that

> "Every one's blood upon end it will stand,
> And the hair run cold in their veins!

And was Dr. Paul out here when California was admitted into the Union, — 1850, wasn't it?"

"Of course; why, my child, he was one of the delegates called by General Riley, the military governor, to meet in convention at Monterey and make a state constitution. That was September, too, — the first day of September,

1849. He went back to the East some time afterwards, and stayed ten or fifteen years; but he was a real pioneer and 'forty-niner' all the same."

The next night, September 9th, was so cool that the camp-fire was more than ordinarily delightful; accordingly they piled on more wood than usual, and prepared for a grand blaze. It was always built directly in front of the sitting-room tent, so that Mrs. Howard and Mrs. Winship could sit there if they liked; but the young people preferred to lie lazily on their cushions and saddles under the oak-tree, a little distance from the blaze. The clear, red firelight danced and flickered, and the sparks rose into the sombre darkness fantastically, while the ruddy glow made the great oak an enchanted palace, into whose hollow dome they never tired of gazing. When the light streamed highest, the bronze green of the foliage was turned into crimson, and, as it died now and then, the stars winked brightly through the thousand tiny windows formed by the interlacing branches.

"Well," said the doctor, bringing his Chinese lounging-chair into the circle, and lighting his pipe so as to be thoroughly happy and comfortable, "will you banish distinctions of age and allow me to sit among you this evening?"

"Certainly," Margery said, "that's the very point of the celebration. This is Admission Day, you know, and why should n't we admit you?"

"True; and having put myself into a holiday humor by dining off Pancho's dish of *guisado* (I suppose to-night of all nights we must call beef and onion stew by its local name), I will proceed to business, and we will talk about California. By the way, I shall only conduct the exercises, for I feel rather embarrassed by the fact that I 've never killed, or been killed by, a bear, never been bitten by a tarantula, poisoned by a rattlesnake, assaulted by a stage-robber, nor anything of that sort. You have all read my story of crossing the plains. I even did that in a comparatively easy and unheroic fashion. I only wish, my dear girls and boys, that we had with us some one of the brave and energetic men and women who made that terrible journey at the risk of their lives. The history of the California Crusaders, the thirty thousand or more emigrants who crossed the plains in '48 more than equals the great military expeditions of the Middle Ages, in magnitude, peril, and adventure. Some went by way of Santa Fé and along the hills of the Gila: others, starting from Red River, traversed the Great Stake Desert and went from El Paso del Norte to Sonora; others went through Mexico, and, after spending over a hundred days at sea, ran into San Diego and gave up their vessels; others landed exhausted with their seven months' passage round the Horn; and some reached the spot on foot after walking the whole length of the California peninsula."

"What privations they must have suffered!" said Mrs. Howard. "I never quite realized it."

"Why, the amount of suffering that was endured in those mountain passes and deserts can never be told in words. Those who went by the Great Desert west of the Colorado found a stretch of burning salt plains, of shifting hills of sand, with bones of animals and men scattered along the trails; of terrible and ghastly odors rising in the hot air from the bodies of hundreds of mules, and human creatures too, that lay half buried in the glaring white sand. A terrible journey indeed; but if any state in the Union could be fair enough, fertile enough, and rich enough to repay such a lavish expenditure of energy and suffering, California certainly was and is the one. Now who can tell us something of the name 'California'? You, Geoffrey?"

"Geoffrey has crammed!" exclaimed Bell maliciously. "I believe he's been reading up all day and told papa what question to ask him!"

"I'll pass it on to you if you like," laughed Geoffrey.

"No,—you'd never get another that you could answer! Go on!"

"In 1534, one Hernando de Grijalva was sent by Hernando Cortez to discover something or other, and it was probably he who then saw the peninsula of California; but a quarter of a century before this a romance called 'Esplandian' had appeared in Spain, narrating the adventures of an Amazonian queen who brought allies from 'the right hand of the Indies' to assist the infidels in their attack upon Constantinople — by the way I forgot to say that she was a pagan. This queen of the Amazons was called Calafia, and her kingdom, rich in gold and precious stones, was named California. The writer of the romance derived this name, perhaps, from Calif, a successor of Mohammed. He says: 'Know that on the right hand of the Indies there is an island named California, very close to the Terrestial Paradise, and it was peopled by black women without any man among them, for they lived in the fashion of the Amazonia. They were of strong and hardy bodies, of ardent courage, and of great force. Their island was the strongest in all the world, with its steep cliffs and rocky shore. Their arms were all of gold, and so was the harness of the wild beasts which they tamed and rode. For in the whole island there was no metal but gold. They lived in caves wrought out of the rocks with much labor, and they had many ships with which they sailed out to other countries to obtain booty.' Cortez and Grijalva believed that they were near the coast of Asia, for they had no conception of the size of the world nor of the vastness of the Pacific Ocean; and as the newly discovered land corresponded with the country described in the romance, they named the peninsula California."

"My book," said Philip, "declared that the derivation of the name was very uncertain, and that it was first bestowed on one of the coast bays by Bernal Diaz."

"Now Philip!" exclaimed Margery, "do you suppose we are going to believe that, after Geoff's lovely story?"

"Certainly not; I only thought I'd permit you to hear both sides. I knew of course that you would believe the prettier story of the two, — girls always do!"

"That is n't a 'pretty story,' your remark I mean, so we won't believe it; will we, girls?" asked Bell.

"Now Polly, your eyes sparkle as if you could n't wait another minute; your turn next," said Dr. Winship.

"I am only afraid that I can't remember my contribution, which is really Bell's and still more really Pancho's, for he told it to us, and Bell translated it and made it into a story. We call it 'Valerio, or the Mysterious Mountain Cave.'"

"Begins well!" exclaimed Jack.

"Now, Jack, you must be nice. Remember this is Bell's story, and she is letting me tell it so that I can bear my share in the entertainment."

"Pancho believes every word of it," added Bell, "and says that his father told it to him; but as I had to change it from bad Spanish into good English, I don't know whether I've caught the idea exactly."

"Oh, it will do quite nicely, I've no doubt," said Jack encouragingly, "we've often heard you do good English into bad Spanish, and turn and turn about is only fair play. Don't mind me, Polly — I will be gentle!"

"Jack, if you don't behave yourself I'll send

you to bed," said Elsie; and he ducked his head obediently into her lap, as Polly, with her hands clasping her knees, and with the firelight dancing over her bright face, leaned forward and told the Legend of

VALERIO, OR THE MYSTERIOUS MOUNTAIN CAVE.

" A long time ago, before the settlement of Santa Barbara by the whites, the Mission *padres* had a great many Indians under their control, who were known as *peons,* or serfs. They were given enough to eat, were not molested by the outside Indians, and were entirely peaceable. There were so few moun- tain passes by which to enter Santa Barbara that they were easily held, and of course the *padres* were anxious to keep their Indians from running away, lest they should show the wilder tribes the way to get in and commit depreda- tions. These peaceable Indians paid tribute to intermediary tribes to hold the passes and do their fighting. Those about the Mission gave corn and cereals and hides and the products of the sea, and got in exchange *piñones* (pine nuts). One of these Indians, named Valerio, was a strong, brave, handsome youth, whose haughty spirit revolted at his servitude, and after seeking an opportunity for many weeks he finally escaped to the Santa Ynez mountains, where he found a cave in which he hid himself, drawing himself up by a rope and taking it in after him. The Indians had unlimited belief in Valerio's mysterious and wonderful powers. Pancho says that he could make himself invisible at will, that locks and keys were powerless against him; and that no one could hinder his taking money, horses, or food. All sorts of things disappeared mysteriously by day and by night, and the robberies were one and all laid to the door of Valerio. But after a while Valerio grew lonely in his mountain retreat. He longed for human companionship, and at length, becoming desperate, he descended on the Mission settlement and kidnapped a young Indian boy named Chito, took him to his cave, and admitted him into his wild and lawless life. But Chito was not contented. He liked home and comfortable slavery better than the new, strange life; so he seized the first opportunity, and being a bright, daring little lad, and fleet of foot, he escaped and made his way to the Mission. Arriving there he told wonderful stories of Valerio and his life; how his marvelous white mare seemed to fly, rather than gallop, and leaped from rock to rock like a chamois; and how they lived upon wheat bread, cheeses,

wine, and other delicacies instead of the coarse
fare of the Indians. He told them the location of the cave and described the way thither;
so the Alcalde (he was the mayor or judge,
you know, Elsie), got out the troops with their
muskets, and the padres gathered the Mission
Indians with their bows and arrows, and they
all started in pursuit of the outlaw. Among
the troops were two *hechiceros* (wizards or medicine men), whose bowed shoulders and griz-
zled beards showed them to be men of many
years and much wisdom. When asked to give
their advice they declared that Valerio could
not be killed by any ordinary weapons, but that
special means must be used to be of any avail
against his supernatural powers. Accordingly
one of the *hechiceros* broke off the head of his
arrow, cast a charm over it, and predicted that
this would deal the fatal blow. The party
started out with Chito as a guide, and after
many miles of wearisome travel, up rugged
mountain sides and over steep and almost im-
passable mountain trails, they paused at the
base of a cliff and saw, far up the height, the
mouth of Valerio's cave, and what was more,
Valerio himself sitting in the doorway fast
asleep. Alas! he had been drinking too heavily of his stolen wine, or he would never have

so exposed himself to the enemy. They fired a
volley at him. One shot only took effect and
even this would not have been possible save
that the spell was not upon him because of his
sleep; but the one shot woke him and, half
rising, he staggered and fell from the mouth
of the cave to a ledge of rocks beneath. He
sprang to his feet in a second and ran like a
deer towards a tree where his white mare was
fastened. They fired another volley, but, though
the shots flew in every direction, Valerio passed
on unharmed; but just as he was disappearing
from view the *hechicero* raised his bow and
the headless arrow whizzed through space and
pierced him through the heart. They clambered up the cliffs with shouts of triumph and
surrounded him on every side, but poor Valerio had surrendered to a more powerful enemy
than they! Wonderful to relate, he still
breathed, though the wound should have been
instantly fatal. They lifted him from the
ground and tied him on his snow-white mare,
his long hair reaching almost to the ground,
his handsome face as pale as death, the blood
trickling from his wound; but the mysterious
power that he possessed seemed to keep him
alive in spite of his suffering. Finally one of
the *hechiceros* decided that the spell lay in the

buckskin cord that he wore about his throat, —
a rough sort of necklace hung with bears'
claws and snake rattles, — and that he never
would die until the magic cord was cut. This,
after some consultation, was done. Valerio
drew his last breath as it parted asunder, and
they bore his dead body home in triumph to
the Mission.

"But he is not forgotten. Stories are still
told of his wonderful deeds, and people still go
in search of money that he is supposed to have
hidden in his cave. The Mexican women who
tell *suertes*, or fortunes, describe the location
of the money; but as soon as any one reaches
the cave he is warned away by a little old man,
who stands in the door and protects the buried
treasure. An Indian lad, who was riding over
the hills one day with his horse and his dogs,
dismounted to search for his moccasin, when he
suddenly noticed that the dogs had chased
something into a cave in the rocks. He followed, and, peering into the darkness, saw two
gleaming eyes. He thrust his knife between
them, but struck the air; and, though he had
been standing directly in front of the opening,
so that nothing could have passed him, yet he
heard the clatter of hoofs and the tinkle of
spurs, and, turning, saw a mysterious horse-

man, whose pale face and streaming hair melted into the mountain mist, as it floated down from the purple Santa Ynez peaks into the lap of the vine-covered foot-hills below."

CHAPTER X.

MORE CAMP-FIRE STORIES.

> " And still they watched the flickering of the blaze,
> And talked together of the good old days."

" BRAVA!" " Bravissima!" " Splendid, Polly!" exclaimed the boys. " Bell, you 're a great author!"

" Could n't have done better myself — give you my word!" cried Jack, bowing profoundly to Bell and Polly in turn, and presenting them with bouquets of faded leaves hastily gathered from the ground.

" Polly covered herself with glory," said the doctor; " and I am very proud of your part in it, too, my little daughter. I have some knowledge of Pancho's capabilities as a narrator, and I think the 'Story of Valerio' owes a good deal to you. Now, who comes next? Margery?"

"No, please," said Margery, "for I have another story. Take one of the boys, and let's have more facts."

"Yes, something historic and profound, out of the encyclopedia, from Jack," said Polly, saucily.

"Thanks, Miss Oliver. With you for an audience any man might be inspired; but" —

"But not a *boy?*"

"Mother, dear, remove that child from my sight, or I shall certainly shake her! Phil, go on, just to keep Polly quiet."

"Very well. Being the oldest Californian present, I" —

"What about Dr. Paul?" asked the irrepressible Polly.

"He wasn't born here," responded Philip, dryly, "and I was."

"I think that's a quibble," interrupted Bell. "Papa was here twenty years before you were."

"It's not my fault that he came first," answered Philip. "Margery and I are not only the oldest Californians present, but the only ones. Isn't that so, sir?"

"Quite correct."

"Oh, if you mean that way, I suppose you

are ; but still papa helped frame the Constitution, and was here on the first Admission Day, and was one of the Vigilantes, — and I think that makes him more of a real Californian than you. You've just 'grown up with the country.' "

" Bless my soul ! What else could I do ? I would have been glad to frame the Constitution, admit the State, and serve on the Vigilance Committee, if they had only waited for me ; but they went straight ahead with the business, and when I was born there was nothing to do but stand round and criticise what they had done, or, as you express it, ' grow up with the country.' Well, as I was saying when I was interrupted," —

" Beg pardon."

" Don't mention it. Uncle Doc has asked me to tell Mrs. Howard and Elsie how they carried on the rodeos ten or fifteen years ago. Of course I was only a little chap " (*"Very* little," murmured his sister), " but never too small to stick on a horse, and my father used often to take me along. The rodeos nowadays are neither as great occasions, nor as exciting ones, as they used to be ; but this is the way a rodeo is managed. When the spring rains are mostly over, and the grass is fine, — say in April, — the ranchero of a certain ranch sends word to all his neighbors that he will hold a rodeo on a certain day or days. Of course the cattle used to stray all over the country, and get badly mixed, as there were no fences; so the rodeo was held for the purpose of separating the cattle and branding the calves that had never been marked.

"The owners of the various ranches assemble the night before, bringing their vaqueros with them. They start out very early in the morning, having had a cup of coffee, and ride to the 'rodeo-ground,' which is any flat, convenient place where cañons converge. Many of the cattle on the hills round about know the place, having been there before, and the vaqueros start after them and drive them to the spot."

"How many vaqueros would there be?" asked Elsie.

"Oh, nine or ten, perhaps; and often from one thousand to three thousand cattle, — it depends on the number of ranches. and cattle represented. Some of the vaqueros form a circle round the cattle that they have driven to the rodeo-ground, and hold them there while others go back to the ranch for breakfast and fresh horses."

"Fresh horses so soon?" said Mrs. Howard.

" I thought the mustangs were tough, hardy little beasts, that would go all day without dropping."

" Yes, so they are; but you always have to begin to 'part out' the cattle with the freshest and best-trained horses you have. The owners and their best vaqueros now go into the immense band of cattle, and try to get the cows and the unbranded calves separated from the rest. You can imagine what skillful engineering this takes, even though you never saw it. Two work together; they start a certain cow and calf and work them through the band of cattle until they near the outside, and then 'rush' them to a place three or four hundred yards beyond, where other vaqueros are stationed to receive and hold them. Of course the cattle don't want to leave the band, and of course they don't want to stay in the spot to which they are driven."

" I don't blame them!" cried Bell impetuously. " Probably the cows remember the time when they were branded themselves, and they don't want their dear little bossies put through the same operation."

" Very likely. Then more cows and calves are started in the same way; the greatest difficulty being had with the first lot, for the cattle always stay more contentedly together as the group grows larger. Occasionally one ' breaks ' and runs off on the hills, and a vaquero starts after him, throws the reata and lassos him, or ' lass's ' him, as the California boys say."

" There must be frightful accidents," said Mrs. Winship.

" Yes; but not so many as you would suppose, for the horsemanship, in its particular way, is something wonderful. When an ugly steer is lassoed and he feels the reata or lariat round his neck, he sometimes turns and ' makes ' for the horse, and unless the vaquero is particularly skillful he will be gored and his horse too ; but he gives a dexterous turn to the lariat, the animal steps over it, gets tangled and thrown. Frequently an animal breaks a horn or a leg. Sometimes one fall is not enough, — the steer jumps up and pursues the horse. Then the vaquero keeps a little ahead of him and leads him back to the rodeo ground where another vaquero lassos him by the hind legs and throws him, while the reata is taken off his neck."

" There is another danger too," added Dr. Winship. " The vaquero winds the reata very tightly round the pommel of his saddle to hold the steer, and he is likely to have his finger caught in the hair rope and cut off."

"Yes, I forgot that. Two or three of the famous old vaqueros about Santa Barbara — José María, José Antonio, and old Clemente, — have each lost a finger. Well, the vaqueros at length form in a circle round the band of selected cattle. The ranch owner who gives the rodeo takes his own cattle that he has found, — the ones bearing his brand you know, — and drives them in with the ones to be branded, leaving in the rodeo-ground the cattle bearing the brands of all the other rancheros. There has been much drinking of *aguardiente* (brandy) and everybody by this time is pretty reckless. Then they drive this selected band to the home corral, the vaqueros yelling, the cattle 'calling,' and the reatas whizzing and whistling through the air. If any unfortunate tries to escape his fate he is pursued, 'lass'd,' and brought back. By this time the cattle are pretty well heated and angry, and when they get into the crowded corral they horn each other and try to gore the horses. A fire is then built in one corner of the corral and the branding-irons are heated."

"Oh! hold my hand, Polly, if the branding is going to begin, I hate it so," exclaimed Elsie.

"I won't say much about it, but it's no worse

than a thousand things that people have to bear every year of their lives. Animals never have to have teeth filled, for instance, nor limbs amputated " —

" Oh, just think of a calf with a wooden leg, or a cow with false teeth! Would n't it be funny?" laughed Bell.

" They don't have a thousand ills that human flesh is heir to, so they must be thankful they get off so easy. Well! the branding-irons are heated, as I say, — each cattle owner having his special brand, which is properly recorded, and which may be any device not previously used.

Two men now catch the calves; one lassoing them by the head, the other by the legs. A third man takes the iron from the fire and brands the chosen letter or hieroglyphic on the animal's hind quarter."

" Sometimes on the fore quarter, don't they?" asked Bell. " I 've seen brands there, — your horse has two, and our cow has one also."

" Yes, a brand on the fore quarter shows that the animal has been sold, but it always has the original brand on the hind quarter. When a sale is effected, the new brand is put anywhere in front of the fifth rib, and this constitutes what they call a *venta*, or sale. If you notice some of the little 'plugs' ridden by Santa Barbara boys, you'll see that they bear half a dozen brands. By the way, if the rodeo has been a very large one they are several days branding the cattle, so they are turned out to *pastorear* a little while each day."

"The brand was absolute sign of ownership you know, girls," said Dr. Winship, "and though there was the greatest care exercised in choosing and recording the brands, there was plenty of opportunity for cheating. For instance, a man would often see unbranded cattle when riding about, and there was nothing to prevent his dismounting, building a fire, heating his iron, and putting his own brand on them. Then, at the next rodeo, they were simply turned over to him, for, as I say, the brand was absolute ownership."

> "When e'er I take my rides abroad,
> How many calves I see.
> And as I brand them properly
> They all belong to me,"

said Bell.

"How I should like to see a rodeo," sighed Elsie. "I can't imagine how the vaqueros can fling the reata while they are riding at full speed."

"It is n't so very wonderful," said Polly nonchalantly; "the most ordinary people can learn it; why! your brother Jack can lasso almost as well as a Mexican."

"And I can 'lass' any stationary object myself," cried Bell, — "a hitching post, or even a door knob; I can do it two or three times out of ten."

"That shows immense skill," answered Jack, "but as the thing you want to 'lass' never does stay still, and as it is absolutely necessary to catch it more than three times out of ten, you probably would n't make a name and fortune as a vaquero. Juan Capistrano, by the way, used to be famous with the lariat. I had heard of his adventure with a bull on the island of Santa Rosa, and I asked him about it to-day; but he had so exhausted himself telling stories to Bell that he had very few words for me. You see there was a bull, on Santa Rosa island, so wild that they wanted to kill him; but nobody could do it, though he was a terror to any one who ventured on the island. They called him 'Antiguelo,' because of his long horns and long tail. He was such a terrible fighter that all the vaqueros were afraid to lass' him, for he always broke away with the lariat. You see a horse throws a bull by skill and not by strength, of course. You can choke almost any bull; but this one was too smart! he would crouch on his haunches and pull back until the rope nearly choked him and then suddenly 'make' for the horse. Juan Capistrano had a splendid horse — you see as much depends on the horse as the man in such a case — and he came upon Antiguelo on the Cerro Negro and lass'd him. Well, did he fight? I asked. *'Si, Señor.'* Well, what happened? *'Yo lo maté'* (I killed him), he said, with a shrug of his shoulders, and that's all I could get out of Juan regarding his adventure."

"But you have n't done your share, you lazy boy," objected Bell. "You must tell us more."

"What do you want to hear? I am up on all the animal and vegetable life of Southern California, full of interesting information concerning its old customs, can give you Spanish names for all the things that come up in ordinary conversation, and am the only man present who can make a rawhide reata," said Jack, modestly.

"Go on and tell us how, O great and wise *reatero*," said Bell.

"I'll tell you that myself," said Elsie, "for

I 've seen him do it dozens of times, when he should have been studying his little lessons. He takes a big piece of rawhide, cuts a circle right out of the middle, and then cuts round and round this until he has one long continuous string, half an inch wide. He then stretches it and scrapes the hair off with a knife or a piece of glass, gets it into four strands, and braids it ' round.' "

" Perhaps you think braiding ' round ' is easy to do," retorted Jack, in an injured tone, " but I know it took me six months to learn to do it well."

" I fail to see," said his mother, " how a knowledge of ' braiding round ' and lassoing of wild cattle is going to serve you in your university life and future career."

" Oh, yes, it will. I shall be the Buffalo Bill of Harvard, and I shall give charming little entertainments in my rooms, or in some little garden-plot suitable to the purpose."

" Shall you make a point of keeping up with your class ? " asked Mrs. Winship.

" Oh, yes, unless they go too fast. My sports won't take any more time than rowing or base ball. They 'll be a little more expensive, because I 'll have to keep some wild cattle constantly on hand, and perhaps a vaquero or two; but a vaquero won't cost any more than a valet."

"I did n't intend furnishing you with a valet," remarked his mother.

"But I shall be self-supporting, mother dear. I shall give exhibitions on the campus, and the gate money will keep me in luxury."

"This is all very interesting," said Polly, cuttingly, "but what has it to do with California, I 'd like to know?"

"Poor dear! Your brain is so weak. Can't you see that when I am the fashion in Cambridge, it will be noised about that I gained my marvelous skill in California? This will increase emigration. I don't pretend to say it will swell the population like the discovery of gold in '48, but it will have a perceptible effect."

"You are more modest than a whole mossy bank of violets," laughed Dr. Paul. "Now, Margery, will you give us your legend?"

"Mine is the story of Juan de Dios (literally, Juan of God), and I 'm sorry to say that it has a horse in it, like Polly's; only hers was a snow-white mare, and mine is a coal-black charger. But they would n't tell us any romantic love stories; they were all about horses."

STORY OF JUAN DE DIOS.

"In early days, when Americans were coming in to Santa Barbara, there were many cattle buyers among them; and there were large bands of robbers all over the country who were ready to pounce on these travelers on their way to the great cattle ranchos, kill them, and steal their money and clothes, as well as their horses and trappings. No one could understand how the robbers got such accurate information of the movements of the travelers, unless they had a spy somewhere near the Mission, where they often stopped for rest and refreshment.

"Now, there was a certain young Indian vaquero in the employ of the padres at La Mission de la Purísima. He was a wonderful horseman, and greatly looked up to by his brother vaqueros, because he was so strong, alert, and handsome, and because he was always dressed elegantly in rich old Spanish embroideries and velvets, given to him, he said, by men for whom he had done great services.

"One day a certain traveler, a Spanish official of high degree, came from Monterey to wed his sweetheart, the daughter of the richest cattle owner in all the country round. His spurs and bit and bridle were of solid silver; his *jaquima* (halter) was made of a hair rope whose strands had been dyed in brilliant colors; his *tapaderos* (front of the stirrups), *mochilas* (large leather saddle flaps), and *sudaderos* (thin bits of leather to protect the legs from sweat), were all beautifully stamped in the fashion used by the Mexicans; his saddle blankets and his housings were all superb, and he wore a broad sombrero encircled with a silver snake and trimmed with silver lace.

" The traveler stayed at La Purísima all night, and set out early in the morning to ride the last forty miles that separated him from his bride. But Juan and two other robbers were lying in wait for him behind a great rock that stood at the entrance of a lonely cañon. They appeared on horseback, one behind the unfortunate man and two in front, so that he could escape neither way. They finally succeeded in lassoing the horse and throwing him to the ground with his rider, who defended himself bravely with his knife, but was finally killed and robbed, Juan taking his clothes and trappings, and the other two dividing the contents of his purse. They could not have buried their victim as successfully as usual, or else they were surprised, and had to escape, for the body was

found ; and Juan, whom the padres had begun
to view with suspicion, was nowhere to be found
about the Mission. Troops were sent out in
pursuit of him, for this particular traveler was
a high official, and it was necessary that his
death should be avenged. They at last heard
that Juan had been seen going towards Santa
Ynez Mission, and, pursuing him thither, they
came upon him as he was driving a band of
horses into a corral, and just in the act of
catching his own horse, a noble and powerful
animal, called Azabache, because of his jet-
black color. The men surrounded the corral,
and ordered him to surrender. He begged
them to wait until he had saddled Azabache,
and then they might shoot them both down
together. He asked permission to call three
times (*pegar tres gritos*), and after the
third call they were to shoot. His last wish
was granted. He saddled and mounted his
splendid horse, called once — twice — thrice, —
but when the last shout faded in the air, and
the troops raised their muskets to fire, behold,
there was no Juan de Dios to be seen. They
had been surrounding the corral so that no one
could have ridden out ; they looked among the
horses, but Azabache was nowhere to be found.

"Just then a joyous shout was heard, so

ringing and triumphant that every man turned in the direction from which it came. There, galloping up the hillside, nearly half a mile distant, was Juan de Dios, mounted on his coal-black Azabache! But it was no common sunshine that deepened the gorgeous colors of his trappings and danced upon his silver spurs till they glistened like two great stars! It was a broad, glittering stream of light such as no mortal had ever seen before and which almost blinded the eyes; and over this radiant path of golden sunbeams galloped Juan de Dios, until he disappeared over the crest of the mountain. Then the light faded: the padres crossed themselves in silence and went home to their Mission! and Juan de Dios never was heard of more."

Modest little Margery was hailed with such cheers that you could not have seen her cheeks for the blushes; and, just as the party began to think of forsaking the fascinating camp-fire for bed, Bell jumped up impetuously and cried, "Here Philip, give me the castanets, please. Polly and Jack, you play 'Las Palomas' for me and I'll sing and show you the dance of that pretty Mexican girl whom I saw at the ball given under the Big Grape Vine. Wait till I take off my hair ribbon, — lend me your scarf, mamma, — now begin!'"

LAS PALOMAS.*
(THE DOVES.)

Cua - tro pa - lo - mi - tas blan - cas que vie -
nen de por a - llá.   U - nas á las o - tras
di - cen no hay a - mor como el de a - cá.

It is barely possible, but not likely, that anything prettier than Bell's Mexican *danza* was to be seen under the light of the September stars that night; although they were doubtless shining down upon a thousand lovely things. With all the brightness of her loosened hair rising and falling with the motion of her swaying figure, — with her twinkling feet, her crimson cheeks and parted lips, she looked the very spirit of the dance, and her enraptured audience only allowed her to stop when she was absolutely breathless.

"Oh! what a beautiful evening!" exclaimed

* Four little white doves began to coo,
  To coo to their mates so fair;
  And each to the other dove said "your coo
  With mine cannot compare!"

Elsie, when the celebration was finally over. " Was there ever such a dear, dear cañon with such dear people in it! If it only would n't rain and we could live here forever!"

> " Rain, rain, stay away!
> Come again another day,
> Little Elsie wants to play,"

recited Polly, and then everybody went to their straw beds.

CHAPTER XI.

BREAKING CAMP.

"The thirsty earth soaks up the rain
And drinks and gapes for drink again;
The plants suck in the earth and are,
With constant drinking, fresh and fair."

BUT it did rain; and it did n't wait until they were out of the cañon, either. It began long before the proper time, and it by no means confined itself to a shower, but opened the winter season fully a month before there was any need of it, and behaved altogether in a most heartless and inconsiderate manner, like a very spoil-sport of a rain.

It began after dark, so as to be just as disagreeable as possible, and under the too slight cover of their tents the campers could hear the rush and the roar of it like the tramping of myriad feet on the leaves. Pancho and the two Chinamen huddled under the broad syca- mores in their rubber blankets, and were dry and comfortable; but all the waterproof tents leaked, save Elsie's.

But when it was dawn, the Sun, having heard nothing apparently of any projected change in the weather, rose at the usual time in the most resplendent fashion, — brighter, rosier, and more gloriously, if you will believe me, than he had risen that whole long sunshiny summer! And he really must have felt paid for getting up at such an unearthly hour in the morning, when, after he had clambered over the gray mountain peaks, he looked down upon Las Flores Cañon, bathed in the light of his own golden beams.

If he knew anything about Ancient History and Biblical Geography, — and if he did n't I don't know who should, inasmuch as he had been present from the beginning of time, — he must have thought it as fair as the Garden of Eden; for Nature's face simply shone with cleanliness, like that of a smiling child just fresh from its bath, and every leaf of every tree glistened as he beamed upon it, and shook off its crystal drops that he might turn them into diamonds.

"It was only a shower," said Dr. Winship, as he seated himself on a damp board and partook of a moist breakfast, "and with this sun the tents will be dry before night; Elsie has caught no cold, the dust will be laid, and we can stay another week with safety."

Everybody was hilarious over this decision save the men-of-all-work, who longed unspeakably for a less poetic existence, — Hop Yet, particularly, who thought camping out "not muchee good."

Dicky was more pleased than anybody, perhaps, as every day in the cañon was one day less in school; not that he had ever been to school, but he knew in advance, instinctively, that it would n't suit him. Accordingly he sought the wettest possible places and played all day with superhuman energy. He finally found Hop Yet's box of blueing under a tree, in a very moist and attractive state of fluidity, and just before dinner improved the last shining hour by painting himself a brilliant hue and appearing at dinner in such a fiendish guise that he frightened the family into fits.

Now Dr. Winship was one of the most

weather-wise men in California, and his predic-
tions were always quite safe and sensible; but
somehow or other it did rain again in two or
three days, and it poured harder than ever,
too. To be sure, it cleared promptly, but the
doctor was afraid to trust so fickle a person as
the Clerk of the Weather had become, and
marching orders were issued.

The boys tramped over all their favorite bits
of country, and the girls visited all their best
beloved haunts, every one of them dear from a
thousand charming associations. They looked
for the last time in Mirror Pool, and saw the
reflection of their faces, — rather grave faces
just then, over the leave-taking.

The water-mirror might have been glad to
keep the picture forever on its surface, — Margery with her sleek braids and serene forehead;
Polly, with saucy nose and mischievous eyes,
laughing at you like a merry water-sprite;
Bell, with her brilliant cheeks glowing like two
roses just fallen in the brook; and Gold Elsie,
who, if you had put a frame of green leaves
about her delicate face and yellow locks, would
have looked up at you like a water-lily.

They wafted a farewell to Pico Negro, and
having gotten rid of the boys, privately embraced a certain Whispering Tree under whose

singing branches they had been wont to lie and listen to all the murmuring that went on in the forest.

Then they clambered into the great thorough-brace wagon, where they all sat in gloomy silence for ten minutes, while Dicky's tan terrier was found for the fourth time that morning; and the long train, with its baggage carts, its saddle horses and its dogged little pack mules, moved down the rocky steeps that led to civilization. The gate that shut them in from the county road and the outer world was opened for the last time, and shut with a clang, and it was all over, — their summer in a cañon !